JUST ANNOYING!

Is this the right book for you?
Take the ANNOYING TEST and find out.

YES **NO**

❏ ❏ Do you ask "Are we there yet?"
over and over on long car trips?

❏ ❏ Do you like to drive people crazy by
copying everything they say and do?

❏ ❏ Do you hog the shower
and use up all the hot water?

❏ ❏ Do you enjoy asking silly questions
that have no real answers?

❏ ❏ Do you swing on the clothesline
whenever you get the chance?

SCORE: One point for each "yes" answer.
3–5 You are obviously a very annoying person.
You will love this book.

1–2 You are a fairly annoying person.
You will love this book.

0 You don't realize how much fun
being annoying can be.
You will love this book.

Also by Andy Griffiths

Just Joking!
The Day My Butt Went Psycho!

VISIT ANDY AT HIS
WEBSITE!
www.andygriffiths.com.au

ANDY GRIFFITHS

JUST Annoying!

WITH ILLUSTRATIONS BY TERRY DENTON.

Scholastic Inc.

New York Toronto London Auckland Sydney
Mexico City New Delhi Hong Kong Buenos Aires

ISBN 0-439-42471-2

12 11 10 9 8 7 6 5 4 3 2 1   3 4 5 6 7 8/06

Printed in the U.S.A.   40
First Scholastic paperback printing, December 2003

Contents

ARE WE THERE YET?

ad?"

"Yes?"

"Are we there yet?"

"No."

"Now?"

"No."

"Now?"

"For goodness sakes!" growls Dad. "Will you stop it!"

"Alright," I say. "Don't get your knickers in a knot."

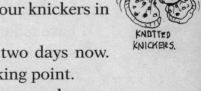

KNOTTED KNICKERS.

We've been in the car for two days now. Mom and Dad are at the breaking point.

Don't get me wrong. I don't *want* them to get mad at me — it just happens.

INTERACTIVE MOVIE!
Grasp book edge between thumb and forefinger and FLIP.

FAVORITE
FLY
RESTING
SPOTS.

Like it or not, when you go on a long car trip, there are times when you just have to stop.

And my parents do not like it.

But what's the alternative?

Do they want me to starve to death? To wet my pants? To be sick all over the backseat?

I think any of these would be a lot more annoying and inconvenient than the few stops it takes to prevent them. I'm actually doing them a favor.

Mom and Dad should save their energy for really annoying things. Like the fly that has been buzzing around in the car for the last half hour. It's driving me crazy. I'm going to do us all a big favor. I'm going to get rid of it.

I roll down the window. The fly jumps away.

It's hiding, just waiting for me to roll the window back up again.

BABY
WILL JUST
LOVE YOUR
OLD DEAD
FLIES

I have to lure it out.

I start doing my best fly-call.

"Bzzzz! Bzzzzzzz! Bzzzzzzzzzzzz!"

Still no fly. Have to do it louder.

"BZZZZZZ! BZZZZZZZZ! BZZZZZZZZZ!"

"Andy!" yells Dad. "I can't concentrate with

BZZZzzz

2

you making that stupid noise. Do you want us to have an accident? Do you want us all to get killed?"

I hate it when Dad asks dumb questions like that. What does he expect me to say? "Yes, Dad, I want us to have an accident. I want us all to get killed."

But I don't say that. It might cause Dad to have an accident. We might all get killed.

"Alright, Dad," I say instead. "Don't get your knickers in a knot."

"And stop telling me not to get my knickers in a knot!" he explodes.

"Okay," I say. "Don't get your trousers in a twist."

Dad hunches over the steering wheel. His knuckles whiten. Tiny drops of perspiration appear on the back of his neck.

He knows he's been outsmarted once again. It must be frustrating for him to have a son as clever as me. It must be hard knowing that he can never win.

The fly lazily cruises in front of my eyes. It's asking for trouble. Well, it's come to the right man.

I once saw a movie where the door of an airplane opened in midair and everybody was

Tying your knickers in knots.
Lesson: 12
The double overhand knot.
1. Take a large pair of knickers.
2.
3.
Put them on.

FAVORITE FLY RESTING SPOTS

  3

To accompany the MOVIE try making your own sound effects.

sucked out by the vacuum it created. I don't need a vacuum quite that powerful, but maybe if I open and close the door, I'll be able to create one strong enough to suck the fly out.

I squeeze the door handle as carefully and slowly as I can so that it doesn't make any noise. I swing it open, then shut.

Open, shut.

Open, shut.

"What do you think you're doing?" screams Dad.

"I'm creating a vacuum," I say.

"What?"

"A vacuum! I'm trying to get a fly out of the car."

"Shut the door! And keep it shut!" shouts Dad. "I'm warning you. If you don't behave yourself, I'll stop the car and you can get out and walk. Do you understand?"

"But, Dad . . ." I say.

"No buts! Do you understand?"

"Yes, Dad."

Dad's knuckles are really white now. He's gripping the steering wheel so hard that his bones are practically breaking through his skin.

I hear a buzz. It's coming from behind me.

NO, WE ARE NOT NEARLY THERE YET!

FOR THE WORLD'S BEST ANNOYING TRICK TURN TO PAGE 38.

ARE WE NEARLY THERE, YET?

Wake up!
This is a story about a fly.

4

DO NOT TURN OVER THIS PAGE DANGER FRIGHTENING SIGHT!

The vacuum didn't work. I turn around but I can't see the fly. Hold on — the noise is coming from outside.

I undo my seat belt and kneel on the seat to get a better view.

There's this crazy-looking guy riding an old black Harley. He's got a long red beard, a black bowl-shaped helmet, and a pair of old-fashioned plastic riding goggles. They make him look like a fly. And his motorcycle sounds like one. Only much louder.

Suddenly the fly shoots across the window. Showdown time!

I try to cup it in my left hand and hook it out of the window.

That's my plan, anyway.

But the fly has other ideas. It skates across the window to the far corner. And then back again. I'm chasing the fly back and forth across the window when I notice that the biker is making hand signals.

He thinks I'm waving to him!

I wave.

He waves back.

I wave again.

He waves back again.

We're best friends now.

I'm looking for the page of jokes about Mechanical Birds.

FOR ALL MECHANICAL BIRD JOKES, SEE PAGE 79.

Are we nearly there yet?

QUIET, mom!

A fly? This is a story about a fly. WOW!

5

"Stop waving," says Dad. "Sit down and put your seat belt back on."

"But he waved first," I say.

"Don't annoy bikers," says Dad. "I don't want any trouble."

"I'm not annoying him — I was just being friendly."

"Sit down!"

"Okay, okay, don't get your knickers in a knot."

I told you already. Don't put your head out the window.

I give one last wave to Bike-man, but he's pulling into a gas station and doesn't see me.

I feel like I've lost my best friend.

I notice a movement out of the corner of my eye.

HARMONIOUS HAPPY HOLIDAY TIP #4.

When you fill up with

Gas, don't insert the nozzle in your brother's ear.

I look up. The fly is on the roof. It's taunting me. It buzzes again.

"Andy," says Dad, "you're pushing your luck!"

"It wasn't me," I say. "It was the fly!"

I have to get rid of this fly. And quickly. Before it gets rid of me.

I reach up and try to cup it with my hand.

It jumps to the left.

I try again.

It jumps to the right and then heads

I'd love to play the fly in the movie of this book.

6

toward the front windshield, daring me to come after it.

I unbuckle my seat belt and dive into the front seat. I catch the fly in midair.

"HOWZAT?" I yell.

I'm lying with my head in Mom's lap and my legs all over the steering wheel.

Dad slams the brakes on. The car lurches forward.

"Get out!" he says.

"But it's not my fault," I say. "It was the fly."

"I don't care whose fault it was," he says. "Out!"

"But look!"

I open my hand to show Dad the fly and prove that I'm not lying, but my hand is empty. It must have swerved at the last minute. Outsmarted by a fly! I hate that.

"Out," says Dad.

Surely he can't be serious.

ELECTRIC CAR.

"I'm sorry, Dad. . . . I was just trying to get the fly out of the car . . . in case it caused an accident . . ."

"You're the only one who is going to cause an accident," he says. "Out."

"Mom?" I say. "Are you going to let him do this?"

I could be the new Michelle Flyffer!

7

"It's for your own good," she says. "You've got to learn."

I open the door.

"You'll be sorry," I say, "when you come back and find my bones being picked clean by vultures."

"There are no vultures in Australia."

"Kookaburras then."

"Shut the door," says Dad. "You're letting the hot air in."

There's no reasoning with him.

I get out of the car and shut the door slowly.

The wheels of the car spin. I am showered by gravel. I wipe the grit out of my eyes and look for the car. It's gone.

I look down at my shoes. There is a big red bull ant on my toe. I brush it off. Maybe I should try to catch it. I might need it for food.

Nah. I won't have to eat ants. They'll be back. Any second. Five minutes tops. Just enough to give me a scare.

I start walking.

Actually it's quite nice. Fresh air. Blue sky. Space. No grumpy parents.

Five minutes pass.

Another five minutes.

And another five minutes.

CUNNING PLACES TO BE SICK IN THE CAR

1. The little ashtray thing ↓

2. Down your little brother's neck ↓

3. In your shoe (desperate)

4. In the interior light cover.

5. Just swallow it.

Romeo, Romeo, wherefore art thou, Romeo?

8

Where are they?

I sit down.

I should just lie down and die — that would teach them.

The only trouble is that it could take a while because I'm actually feeling pretty healthy.

I hear a droning sound in the distance.

Ha! I check my watch. It took them fifteen minutes to give in and come back and get me. That's really going to teach me a lesson I'll never forget. Not.

But as I listen I notice the drone has a different quality. Throatier. Not the putty-putt-putt sound of Dad's car at all.

It's Bike-man!

I jump up and wave.

He waves back and pulls up alongside me.

He looks even crazier close up. His beard is full of insects. Some of them are still alive.

"Well," he says, "if it isn't my little friend. What are you doing out here all by yourself?"

"My parents threw me out of the car," I say. "They told me I had to walk."

"You like bikes?" he says.

"Are you kidding?"

"Hop on then," he says. "What's your name?"

"Andy. What's yours?"

Tricks to play on a biker when he/she is not looking

1. Squirt silicon in their helmet so it sticks to their head... permanently

2. Stick potatoes up their exhaust pipes.

3. Fill their tires up with water.

Don't worry bikers never get annoyed.

DO BIKIES HAVE A SENSE OF HUMOR?

To be, or not to be? OUCH!

9

"Max. Pleased to meet ya!"

He hands me a helmet.

"Here," he says. "Put this on."

It's just like the one he's wearing.

"Hold on," he says.

"To what?" I yell, but he doesn't hear me above the chugging of his motorcycle.

He gives it full throttle.

My stomach drops as he accelerates up the road.

I grab him around the waist.

Roaring wind. My whole body is shaking and vibrating. I'm freezing. I wish I had more clothes on.

I see Mom and Dad's car in the distance.

"That's them!" I yell into Max's ear.

Max surges forward, the old Harley sucking up the highway like spaghetti.

As we pull closer to the car, I signal to Max to blow his horn to let them know I'm here.

He blasts. I wave. But they don't stop. If anything they seem to speed up.

Maybe Dad thinks Max is just trying to hassle him. They probably don't recognize me with a helmet on.

"Max!" I yell. "Go up next to them. I don't think they realize it's me."

I'm going to sneeze.

10

TURN THE PAGE QUICKLY TO MAKE $1,000,000.

Max pulls up alongside them.

I wave.

Dad just looks straight ahead.

"Hey," I yell. "Stop!"

No reaction.

I wave both hands.

Dad flicks a nervous glance across at me, but he doesn't show any sign of recognition. Instead, he hunches over the wheel and pulls away from us at high speed. Wow! I never knew the car could go so fast. If Dad always drove like that, I wouldn't have so much time to get bored.

Max accepts the challenge. He speeds up, but Dad veers on to the other side of the road to block us. Woah!

But Max knows a few tricks, too.

Max pulls back in and rides up the side of the road that Dad has just vacated.

We're back beside them, on the inside lane this time.

Max turns to me and yells above the roar: "They're not going to stop! You're going to have to jump over to 'em."

He's joking.

He's got to be. Either that or he's completely insane.

DANGER LOW BRIDGE

Aaah. Ahh AHHHH Choooo!!

11

"No way!" I yell. "I'm staying with you."

"Stand up," he says. "I'll go in as close as I can."

He's not joking.

He rides right up beside the car and signals for me to stand.

I kneel on the seat. I hold on to Max's shoulders and pull myself up. My legs are shaking.

There's still a huge gap.

"It's too far!" I yell.

Max edges in as close as he dares.

The roof is only a couple feet away.

My stomach is churning.

I don't want to do this.

I'm too young to die!

I bend down.

SPOT THE DIFFERENCE
How many changes are there between picture A and B.

A.   B.
for answer see Pg62

"I can't do it," I yell in Max's ear.

"You have to," he growls.

"Why can't I stay with you?" I say. "I'll be your apprentice."

He laughs.

"Highway's no place for a nice kid like you. Go back. Finish school."

"I'm not nice," I say. "I'm really annoying."

He laughs again, a scary, high-pitched sort of laugh.

12

SORRY! TOO SLOW

"Jump," he says.

He has a wild look in his eyes. Maybe staying here is not such a great idea after all.

I stand up again. This is freaky.

I take a deep breath. I close my eyes. Clench my fists. I don't know what good clenching my fists is going to be in this situation, but it feels like the right thing to do.

Good-bye cruel world.

The wind picks me up and sends me hurtling sideways.

FLY off THE HANDLE.

Thump!

I land on the car roof. I made it!

Dad starts swerving all over the road. He's trying to shake me off.

I've got to make him realize it's me.

I bang on the roof. Dad swerves harder.

I have an idea.

I edge forward, fingers spread as far apart as they will go.

One mistake and I'm gone.

If I can just let him see it's me, he'll slow down.

I push myself down in front of the windshield.

Mom and Dad freak. Eyes wide. Mouths open.

My head seems to have fallen off

13

WHEN
TRAVELING
ON VACATION
WITH A COW
ON YOUR ROOF

ALWAYS:
A STOP EVERY
2 HOURS TO
GIVE THE COW
EXERCISE.
B STOP EVERY
8 HOURS TO
MILK THE
COW.
C ENGAGE
THE COW
IN REGULAR
CONVERSATION.
D FEED IT
YOUR LITTLE
BROTHER'S
CHIPS.
E GIVE IT
A BLANKET,
IT MAY BE
FRIESIAN.
F

ALLOW IT
TO CALL
HOME
REGULARLY.

Suddenly I go flying forward.

Dad has slammed on the brakes.

I flip over onto my back and grab the antenna to stop myself from sliding off the hood onto the road.

The car stops.

I'm lying on my back staring up at the sky. Panting hard. It's over.

Mom and Dad get out.

I take off my helmet.

"This is the limit, Andy! The absolute limit!" says Dad. "What are you trying to do — get yourself killed?"

More dumb questions.

"No," I say. "I was trying to get back into the car. You threw me out, remember?"

"Yes," says Dad. "To teach you a lesson."

"What sort of lesson is that?" I say. "To abandon me in the middle of nowhere with no food, no water, no map, and no sunscreen?"

"We were going to come back," he says, throwing a glance at Mom. Her cheeks go crimson.

"When?" I say. "On your way home?"

He looks sheepish.

"We were about to come back and get you

What?

14

when the biker started chasing us. I was trying to lead him as far away from you as possible. Some of these characters can be pretty dangerous, you know."

I get into the car.

"I don't want to hear any more excuses, Dad," I say. "You tried to get rid of me. You failed. Let's go."

"We were going to come back," says Dad. "Honest."

He starts the engine. He's feeling bad now. He should be.

We pull out onto the road.

There's an enormous noise outside the car. It's Max. He's riding alongside us. I roll down the window and toss the helmet to him. He catches it with one hand, gives me a big grin, and then rockets off into the distance.

I lean back and sigh. Max is cool. Loony, but cool.

Fly fishing

I'm rolling the window back up when I see the fly.

It's sitting right on top of Dad's head.

"It's all your fault," I say quietly. "I've been abandoned. Almost missed out on my vacation. Risked my life. It's all your fault — and you're going to pay."

15

OK, OK. I give up. So what was it. N.W. You win N.W.

N.W. The NYLON WASHER under the nut that holds the seat to the floor under the carpet, just here under my foot. My turn again.

(Note: Never play I SPY in a car with a 7 year old.)

I sit up close behind Dad. I hold my hands just above his head, ready to smash the fly.

It jumps.

The movement distracts me. I clap Dad over both ears instead.

Oops.

His knuckles whiten.

"Dad, I'm sorry — it was a mistake. See, I was trying to . . ."

Dad stops me.

"It's okay, Andy. You don't have to explain."

"I don't?"

"No. We all make mistakes."

Oh, I get it. Mom and Dad won't try to throw me out of the car again. No matter what I do. They've used their biggest threat and it didn't work. It just made them feel bad.

I sit back in my seat and relax. I close my eyes.

I can do anything now. Anything I want. This might not turn out to be such a boring trip after all. I just have one question.

"Dad?" I say.

"Yes?"

"Are we there yet?"

Copycat from Ballarat

My high heels hurt.
My skirt is too long.
My bra is too big.

But I am beautiful.

And, more important, I am annoying Jen.

I have been copying Jen for two days, and she's ready to kill me.

I have copied her talking. I have copied her walking.

But tonight is the biggest challenge of all.

The school dance.

Tonight I'm not only walking and talking like Jen, but I'm dressed like her as well.

We are walking toward the high school. I

am following a few steps behind her. I swing my arm just like she does. I stick my butt out and sway from side to side. I am doing a brilliant job.

At the foot of the steps, she swings around to face me.

I swing around, too.

"I don't see you!" she says to my back.

"I don't see you!" I say to nobody.

"I don't hear you," she says.

"I don't hear you," I say.

"If you want to make a complete idiot of yourself then fine, go ahead. But the only person you're embarrassing is you. Got it?"

"If you want to make a complete idiot of yourself then fine, go ahead," I mimic. "But the only person you're embarrassing is you. Got it?"

She sighs loudly, turns around, and stomps up the steps.

I sigh loudly, turn around, and stomp up the steps, too.

But it's not easy to stomp in high heels. Halfway up I slip and fall back down the stairs. Darn! Jen didn't slip and fall. It's my first mistake of the night.

I'm trying to pick myself up.

18

"Are you alright?" says a deep voice. "That was a nasty fall."

Oh, no. It's Craig Bennett. Number one school sleaze. The worst thing is that all the girls think he's gorgeous. And doesn't he know it.

He's dressed in a sharp new suit. He reeks of aftershave. He has the top three buttons of his shirt undone. I guess that's so he can show off all three of his chest hairs.

"Here, let me help you," he says.

Before I can say no, he slips his arm around my waist and lifts me up.

He holds me for a second, looking straight into my eyes, before taking his arm away.

What a smooth operator! He makes me want to puke.

"My name's Craig," he says. "What's yours?"

"Andy," I say automatically. D'oh! I'm supposed to be a girl!

"Andy?" says Craig.

"I mean Andrea," I say. "My friends call me Andy."

He smiles.

"That's cute. It suits you."

There's no doubt about it. This guy is good.

CLUNK!!

LEARN
GREAT
DANCE
MOVES

№ 11
The
UMBAWI

1.

2.

3.

4.

5.

6.

"I haven't seen you around before," he says. "Are you new?"

"Yes," I say. "We've just moved here from Ballarat."

"Excellent," says Craig. "May I escort you in?"

All I want to do is to get away from this creep and go and annoy Jen. But then a thought strikes me. Maybe the best way to annoy Jen is not to copy her, but to go to the dance on Craig Bennett's arm. She's as crazy about him as the rest of the girls. When she sees me with him, she'll go nuts!

"Yes, that would be . . . elegant," I say. I think that's what you're supposed to say. I don't know. I've never been in this situation before.

Craig holds out his arm, his elbow bent.

I slip my arm through his and he helps me up the stairs.

Craig opens the door and we walk through.

There's a group of guys hanging around the hallway.

I hear a long low wolf-whistle.

Craig freezes.

He looks in their direction and shakes his head.

Aha! Back in control.

"Kids," he snorts. "They're just kids. Ignore them."

They snicker as we walk past them into the gym.

I look for Jen.

She's standing over near the drinks table with a group of her girlfriends. They are all staring at us. Jen is gaping like a fish. She didn't count on this.

"Would you like a drink?" says Craig.

"Yes, thank you," I say. "That would be elegant."

We move toward the table.

White plastic cups are lined up in rows beside a couple of punch bowls.

"Orange or lemon?" says Craig.

"Surprise me," I say.

Craig picks up two cups and hands one to me. He's about to drink from his cup when I have an idea. I catch hold of his wrist with my free hand and twine my arm around his. We sip our drinks and look deep into each other's eyes. I glance over to make sure Jen is getting all this. She is. She looks furious.

She looked deep into my eyes

She comes over to us.

"Hi, Craig," she says with the sweetest smile. She's almost as good an actor as I am.

Help.

SLURP!

"Hi, Jen," he replies without taking his eyes off mine.

"Who's your friend?" says Jen.

"Her name's Andrea," he says. "She's from Ballarat."

"You can say that again," says Jen, shooting me a very dirty look.

"Huh?" says Craig. "Do you two know each other?"

"You could say that," says Jen.

I shrug.

Buk!

It's time to pluck your eyebrows!

"Let's dance," I say. I have to get him away before Jen blows it. I don't want to let her off the hook too soon. I spent hours getting ready — plucking my eyebrows, getting the stupid wig to sit straight, not to mention stuffing my bra with those little white balls from the beanbag chair. I'm going to make her suffer a while longer.

Is the cup half empty

or half full?

I take Craig's hand and lead him toward the dance floor, but he doesn't need any encouragement. Craig leaps into the center of the room and starts going for it like he's in a boy band.

He's pulling every move in the book. Fist in the air. Leg splits. Pirouettes. Even moonwalking. Doesn't this guy have any shame?

wow! writing!

"Come on," he says. "What are you waiting for? Get down! Woooh!"

The only move I'm capable of right at the moment is to shake my head in disbelief. But head shaking is not exactly a snappy dance move. If I want to keep Craig interested, then I'm going to have to get down and dirty — and pretty fast.

Trouble is, I don't know how.

I've never actually danced before.

I usually spend school dances on the sidelines laughing at everybody else trying to dance.

I don't know the first thing about it.

And then it hits me.

I may not be good at dancing but I am an expert at copying. All I have to do is copy Craig and I'll be fine.

He bends his knees and punches the air. I follow. Simple enough.

He does a little jump and a midair twist and then lands on his knees.

I do the same. Only I don't land on my knees — I still haven't got the hang of these high heels. I fall backward onto my behind.

I hear cheering. A large group has formed around us. How embarrassing. I think the only person more embarrassed than me at this point must be Jen. But I can't back out now.

I pick myself up off the floor.

Craig is on his knees. He's leaning backward, staring at the roof, shoulders pumping.

I have no choice but to do the same.

Only I throw in an extra touch of my own.

As I lean back I thrust my chest out and shake.

More cheers.

Craig is impressed.

He helps me up and then pulls me close to him.

"I haven't known you for very long, Andrea," he says, "but I feel a real connection to you."

"That's nice," I say, trying to pull away from him.

I notice that my dancing has caused some of the beanbag balls to fall out of my bra. They are scattered around my feet.

Craig notices, too.

"I see you've brought some snow with you from Ballarat!"

I giggle girlishly. "Oh, Craig. You're so funny. Would you excuse me while I freshen up?"

"Sure," he says, frowning a little.

SOMETHING TO WEAR TO AVOID BRINGING ATTENTION TO YOURSELF AT A PARTY.

SOME CONVERSATION STARTERS FOR YOUR NEXT PARTY

Hi, I'm A MANIC DEPRESSIVE

I love horses. Are you a horse?

THE BUILDING'S ON FIRE!

24

Time for neck exercises.

He releases his grip on me. I practically run to the bathroom at the far end of the hall.

This will not only give me time to repack my bra, but, more important, give him a bit of time to cool off.

MR. SCRIBBLE IN THE GENTS.

I push open the door of the men's room.

"Hey! You can't go in there," says a teacher on duty.

D'oh! I didn't even think. I'm a girl now. I have to use the ladies' room. No way. It must be crawling with girl germs.

I look behind me.

hand dryer

Craig is still standing in the middle of the dance floor watching me.

I have to go in.

I push open the door. I'm almost knocked backward by the smell of perfume and hairspray.

A group of girls are all gathered around the mirror.

"Did you see them?" says one.

"Who *is* that girl he's with?"

"I don't know," says the first. "But did you see her dancing?!"

They all giggle.

"Craig deserves better than that. He is so great."

Up...down...up...

Help!

25

The door slams shut behind me.

They look up and get quiet.

I duck into the closest stall and lock the door.

I didn't think I was that bad. They're jealous, that's all.

I take my top off and pull my bra straps back onto my shoulder.

More beanbag balls have fallen out of one side than the other. I have to balance them up. I may not be a real girl, but I have my pride.

I hear the group of girls whisper and giggle and then leave the room.

It's safe to come out.

I'm at the basin washing my hands when Lisa Mackney walks in.

She looks even more beautiful than usual. She is so nice. I hope she doesn't recognize me.

I stare down into the basin and pretend not to see her.

"Hi," she says. "You're new, aren't you? My name's Lisa."

"Hi, Lisa," I say. "I'm Andrea."

"I know," she says. "Everybody's talking about you."

"Oh?" I say.

"Yes," she says. "You're a really . . . original dancer."

"Thanks," I say. "But it's hard to dance badly when you're with someone as good as Craig."

Lisa puts her hand on my arm and lowers her voice.

"You mustn't take this the wrong way," she says, "but just be careful. Craig's got a . . . reputation. I wouldn't want you to get hurt."

She lowered her voice

"Thanks," I say. "But it's okay. I can look after myself."

Lisa smiles.

She is so beautiful. If there was one girl I could go out with in the whole school, it would be her.

But she would never bother with anyone like me. Not dressed like this, anyway.

I become aware that I'm staring at her.

"Are you okay?" she says.

"I'm fine," I say. "Just a bit dizzy from the dancing."

"You remind me of someone," she says, studying my face.

"Oh, really?" I say, starting to panic.

"Yeah," she says. "This boy I really like. His name is Andy."

Arrrh! GASP!

OH, OH.

27

She's blushing. My heart is pounding. Could it be? Nah. Of course not. Could it?

"Andy?" I say. "Does he have a sister named Jen?"

"Yes!" she says. "How do you know that?"

"Friends of the family," I say.

"Really!" she says. "So you know Andy?"

"Of course," I say. "He's a really cool guy."

"Yes," says Lisa. "But he can be very immature at times."

"Oh!" I say. "He strikes me as being very mature actually. And *so* good looking!"

"Yes," says Lisa, sighing. "I was hoping he would be here tonight."

"Maybe he'll be here later," I say.

I can't believe what I'm hearing! If only I wasn't dressed up like a girl I could ask her to dance. I have to get home and change before it's too late.

Lisa shrugs. "Maybe."

I dry my sweaty hands on a piece of paper towel.

"I have to get back to the dance," I say. "It was nice to meet you."

"You, too," she says. "I hope we can be really good friends."

The joke that was placed here last friday, has been removed by person ,or persons, unknown. Could they please return it by 5.00 today or face the consequences. Pranks like this are JUST ANNOYING.

28

"Me too," I say.

"And remember what I said about Craig."

"Thanks," I say. "I'll be careful."

I pull open the door and go back out into the hall.

I can't see Craig anywhere. Fantastic.

I just want to get home, get changed, and get back as quickly as I can.

I'm heading toward the exit when I feel a hand on my shoulder.

Mr. SCRIBBLE GOES SURFING

"Hey," says Craig. "Where are you going?"

"I have to go home," I say.

"But it's so early," he says. "How about one more dance? You really set that floor on fire, you know."

Dancing with Craig is the last thing I want to do.

she really set the floor on fire.

"I've got a big day tomorrow," I say.

"But it's Saturday. You can sleep in."

"I have to wash my hair."

"Just one more," he begs.

I get the feeling it's going to be quicker to dance than to argue.

"One more," I say, "and then I really have to go."

He leads me onto the floor. But this time

29

he doesn't go crazy. He puts his hands around my waist and tries to pull me toward him.

I try to pull away but he is strong.

BE A CAT. Lesson 4:

Learn to balance on fence...

(meeow)

OR ELSE

The smell of his aftershave is making me feel sick as we shuffle around the floor.

As we pass the refreshments table, I catch Jen's eye. Help me, I mouth silently. She winks at me. She's enjoying this.

The song finishes.

I pull away from Craig.

"I really have to go now," I say.

Danny comes up to me. He's the last person I want to see.

"May I have this dance?" he asks.

(137H.)

"In your dreams, buddy," says Craig, pushing him away and grabbing me around the waist. "This one's mine."

"No, it's not," I say, jerking out of his grasp.

For a moment Craig is stunned. He is not used to being rejected.

This speech balloon and shadow is all that remains of a now extinct joke.

He grabs my shoulder.

I shrug his hand off.

"Stop it!" I say, turning toward the door.

He reaches out to pull me back. I'm quick. But not quick enough.

PHEW!

30

Craig grabs the back of my dress.

The dress rips right down to my waist, revealing my underpants.

I guess you've probably never had the experience of standing in your sister's bra and your X-Men undies in front of the whole school.

THE TOP HALF OF THIS REALLY FUNNY DRAWING HAS BEEN REMOVED FOR REPAIRS. (We apologize for just being ANNOYING!)

If you have, then I feel very sorry for you. If you haven't, then I don't recommend it.

But my embarrassment doesn't end there.

Without the dress to support it, my bra collapses.

The floor is awash with polystyrene balls.

I try to make a run for the door but I trip on my high heels.

Craig reaches forward to stop me falling. He grabs a handful of my hair. My wig comes off in his hand.

"I knew it was you," says Danny. "I knew it all along."

TRY THIS MAGIC EYE PUZZLE

A pile of scribble.

Craig looks at Danny.

Craig looks at me.

He looks at the wig in his hand.

I start to slide away on my back.

"No hard feelings, Craig?" I say. "Just a little joke."

That was frightening.

31

How
TO
BE A
DOG!

1. Look
enthusiastic

2. When in
doubt,
LICK

3. Don't get
too close
to other
dogs.

4. JUST
DON'T!

(Sniff)

He throws the wig on the floor.

"I'm going to punch your face in," he says.

Craig takes off his jacket and starts rolling up his sleeves as he walks toward me.

Jen runs forward. She grabs his arm.

"Don't do that," she says. "He's not worth it! He's just a kid. Come and have a drink."

He looks at me. He looks at Jen. He looks back at me with such anger in his eyes that I wonder if he'll ever get over it.

"Come on," says Jen.

He turns and allows her to lead him away to the refreshments table, his arm around her waist.

I think he'll get over it.

"I knew it was you," says Danny. "I wasn't fooled for a second. I just asked you to dance for a laugh."

I look up.

Lisa Mackney is looking down at me.

"I can explain," I say.

"Go ahead," she says.

"Um . . . er . . . I . . . ah . . . um . . ."

"You could always try telling the truth," she suggests.

She's right. I never thought of that.

"Um — the truth is that I'm very immature for my age."

"I know," she says. "And you know what else?"

"What?" I ask.

"You have terrible taste in underwear."

Terrible
taste in
Underwear.

I'm getting
bored.
I need some
action!

33

Wish you weren't here

I put my suitcase on top of the bed, flick the locks open, and lift up the lid.

He's lying there. Staring. He never stops. He's been staring at me day and night since I took him from Mrs. Scott's garden a few days ago.

Hands on hips. Little fat belly sticking out of his shirt. And the strangest expression on his face. It could be a smile. It could be a grimace. It's hard to tell.

All I know is that he's not like the other gnomes.

Each year when I come to Mildura to visit my grandparents, I borrow one of the gnomes from Mrs. Scott's garden and bring it with me. I take a photograph of the gnome and send it to Mrs. Scott with a little message on the back saying, "Having a great time! Wish you were here. Love, Gnome."

When I get home from the trip I put the gnome back in her garden — exactly where it was before — and leave Mrs. Scott to figure out how on earth a garden gnome manages to travel three hundred miles north all by itself.

Sometimes I give them to Danny and other friends to take away as well. In a good year, Mrs. Scott's gnomes send her postcards from all around Australia.

I don't just do it for Mrs. Scott's benefit, though. I also do it because I think it's a nice thing to do for the gnomes. It must be pretty boring just standing in the same spot in the same garden day after day.

They've always looked pretty happy to escape. Until now.

I take the gnome out of the suitcase and lay him on the bed. I rummage through my clothes to find my shorts. I undo the top button of my jeans and unzip my fly. I stop. The gnome is still staring. I turn him over so that he's face down on the bed.

I know it's stupid to be embarrassed about getting changed in front of a concrete gnome,

I'm a chicken!

but it just doesn't feel right — not the way this gnome stares.

A loud whining noise comes from the backyard.

I go outside.

Grandpa is standing next to what looks like a mini rocket launcher.

"Hey, Andy!" he calls. "Come and see my new mulcher."

Every time I visit, Grandpa's got some new garden machine or gadget. His shed looks like a garden supplies warehouse.

"It can chew anything," he says. "Watch!"

He picks up a branch thicker than his arm. He flicks the switch and the engine roars into action. Grandpa shoves the branch into the blades. There's a high-pitched whining noise. An explosion of sawdust from the exit chute. No more branch.

"Isn't she great?" says Grandpa. His red face is beaming with pride. "Want to try?"

"Yeah," I say.

He hands me a branch. Gray, knotty, and gnarled. I jab the end into the blades. It makes a slight whining noise. I pull back.

"Don't be shy," says Grandpa. "Push like you mean it."

I push the branch in hard. Whine, spit, puff! Gone.

"Want to do another?" he asks, beaming.

"Yeah," I say.

Grandpa hands me another branch. I push it in. Gone! He hands me another. Gone! And another. Gone!

Grandma sticks her head out of the window.

"There'll be nothing left in the backyard if you carry on at that rate," she says. "Why don't you go to the pool, Andy?"

It's not a bad idea. Grandpa's mulcher is fun, but it's hot work.

"Okay, Gran," I say. "Can we do some more later, Grandpa?"

"Yes," he chuckles. "I'll cut down another tree. That should keep us going."

I go back to my bedroom to get my towel.

The gnome is lying on top of the bed.

But not face down like I left him. He's face up. Staring.

That's weird.

But hang on. My suitcase, which was open, has been closed and placed neatly at the foot of the bed. Grandma must have come

WIN FABULOUS PRIZES. 500 PRIZES To Be WON! Count how many times the PAGE NUMBER FLY claims to be a CHICKEN. Check the whole book. then write the number on the back of a SSAE (stamped self addressed envelope)... then POST it, together with your headsize to: see pg 73. DO IT NOW.

into the room while I was outside and straightened things up.

But the gnome is starting to freak me out. I'm going to take the photograph, then wrap him up and try to forget about him so that I can enjoy the rest of my vacation.

I grab my bathing suit, my camera, the gnome, and head for the pool.

THERE'S HEAPS OF PEOPLE AT THE SWIMMING POOL.

The WORLD'S BEST ANNOYING TRICK... Had to be moved to Pg 60.

We apologize for the inconvenience

There's tons of people at the swimming pool.

The diving board is working overtime. Dives, cannonballs, belly flops, screams . . .

Hey! I could set the gnome up on the edge of one of the diving boards. It would make a cool photo.

I wonder if it's against the pool rules?

There's a sign forbidding everything else: no running, no jumping, no horseplay. It doesn't say anything about gnomes, though.

I join the line for the ladder to the highest diving board. I'm holding the gnome under one arm and have my camera over my shoulder.

I hear laughter behind me. I turn around.

Two big guys are smirking.

"Got your gnome, have ya?"

I'm a fly

They crack up laughing.

"Yeah," I say.

"Or is it your little brother?" says one.

"Nah, couldn't be," says the other. "It's too good looking."

This cracks them up again. I ignore them. I put my hand on the thin steel of the ladder and pull myself up. My hand is shaking.

I have to admit that I'm not really a high-diving board sort of guy. I'm more of a bottom-runger. I usually just put my foot on the first step of the ladder and then take it off again and go and play in the kiddie pool. I don't really deal with heights very well. But the smirking guys are behind me. I can't back out now. And besides, I want that photograph.

My knuckles whiten as I climb. My knees feel weak, like they'll cave in if I put too much pressure on them.

Finally I reach the platform. It's so high I can practically see the whole town.

The girl in front of me runs along the plank and then cannonballs to the water below. She screams the whole way down. It's horrible.

Now it's just me and the smirkers.

WARNING
DO NOT
PRESS
THIS
BELL.
It is wired
up to ANDY's
earlobes
and you will
send a 4000
wake up call
to him.
SO JUST
DON'T DO IT

You must
have been
a beautiful
maggot.

I'm a CHICKEN
39

for those who
always open
a book at pg 39
and start
reading, don't
be fooled. The
PAGE NUMBER
FLY wants you
to think he's
a chick, but
he isn't. Oh?

INTRODUCING
NOVELTY
GNOMES

PUNK
GNOME

HAIRY
GNOME

POST
MODERN
GNOME

BUDGET
GNOME

GNOME
SWEET
GNOME.

"Can you give me a second?" I say. "I need to take a picture."

I tiptoe out as far along the plank as I dare. I feel sick. I set the gnome up on the end with its back to the water.

I return to the platform. I kneel down and point my camera at the gnome. I can hardly hold the camera still enough to take the photo.

"Smile," says one of the smirkers.

"He looks like he's in pain," says the other.

"Maybe his pants are too tight."

They crack up laughing again. Maybe *their* pants are too tight.

I take a few shots and tiptoe back out onto the plank to retrieve my gnome. I crouch down to pick him up. I'm trying not to look at the pool below in case I get any more dizzy than I already am. I place my hand on his hat. As I stand up, he seems to jump.

I lose my balance and slip. I grab the end of the diving board. I'm hanging by one hand. The gnome has fallen over onto his side. His head is sticking over the edge of the board. Staring at me. But it's not a look of pain on his face anymore. That's a smile.

I'm slipping. I'm only holding on by two fingers.

Oops.

Make that one finger.

I can't hold on anymore. I'm falling. I hit the water belly first. But I'm alive. I push my way back up to the surface. Spitting and choking.

I look back up at the board.

The gnome is plummeting toward me. He's not content with making me fall, now he's trying to knock me out. He wants to drown me.

WHOOOMP!

The gnome does a fantastic cannonball into the center of the pool and sinks straight to the bottom.

A woman starts screaming and pointing at me.

"Guard! A small child has fallen into the pool!"

"I'm not that small," I call.

The guard dives into the pool. But he doesn't try to save me. He dives down to the bottom of the pool and emerges with the gnome in his hand.

He is not happy.

"Is this yours?" he asks.

"Yes," I say.

WIN FABULOUS PRIZES!
(continued from Pg 73)
...A FROZEN CHICKEN CAR.
Yes, it's your lucky day.
The Frozen CHICKEN CAR (FCC is yours.
A choice of 3 colours (white, black or Rhode Is. red)
2 models (Roaster or boiler).
2nd with or without chips.
BUK BUK

Fly I'm a Fly

41

"Would you mind explaining what he's doing in here?"

"Swimming?" I say.

"Do you realize that garden gnomes are banned from the pool?" he says.

"It doesn't say that on the sign," I say.

"It shouldn't have to," he says. "It should be obvious."

He hands it back to me.

"Get rid of him."

The smirkers are laughing as I leave.

Maybe this whole thing was their fault. Maybe I fell off the diving board because they bounced on it while I was trying to get the gnome. Maybe it was them who kicked it off afterward. Maybe I'm just being paranoid.

Maybe.

SWIMMING POOL GNOME.

KILLER GNOMES

I'm lying in bed.

The night is still and hot.

I can't sleep.

I hear the high-pitched whine of an approaching mosquito. I wait until it gets really loud. It stops. I can feel it on my forehead. I bring my hand up slowly. I whack my head with my open palm. The whining starts up

FLY CHOOK

42

again as the mosquito retreats to the ceiling. Just like the other forty times.

I can't stop thinking about the gnome.

Before I went to bed I wrapped him in a plastic bag and fastened it with fat rubber bands. I buried him down at the bottom of my suitcase under all my clothes. I locked the suitcase and pushed it under the bed.

He would have to be Houdini to get out of there.

But I'm still scared.

He tried to kill me this afternoon. I think. In fact, I'm positive. Sort of.

I hear a noise.

It sounds like somebody knocking.

"Come in," I call.

But nobody comes.

I hear the knocking again. I get out of bed and open the door. Nobody there. Am I going crazy?

I get back into bed.

More knocking.

It's not the door at all.

It's coming from under the bed.

I hear the locks of the suitcase click open.

I can't believe it.

This is crazy.

NAUGHTY
GNOMES
HOW
TO
DISCIPLINE
THEM.

1. Speak
to them
firmly.

2. Slap
them on
the nose.

3. If the
behavior
is repeated,
then speak
to them
VERY firmly.

4. If the
behavior
is repeated
insert gnome
in compost
bin.

5. Buy new
gnome.

43

A concrete garden gnome wrapped in plastic secured by fat rubber bands cannot open a suitcase. Especially not from the inside.

I close my eyes and try to go back to sleep.

But I can't sleep.

I hear rustling.

This is ridiculous.

I grab my flashlight and jump out of bed. I shine the flashlight under the bed at my suitcase. It's locked. I knew I was imagining it. I just had to check.

I switch off the flashlight and get back into bed.

I turn onto my side and try to relax.

I'm just on the edge of falling asleep when I hear the mosquito.

I swipe at it. Miss. It returns. I swipe again. The back of my hand hits something hard under the sheet. I pull the sheet back. It's the gnome. Lying on his side. Staring at me.

I grab him and throw him against the wall with superhuman strength.

The gnome bounces off the wall and lands back on the bed.

I pick him up again and throw him even harder.

This time he doesn't return.

I grab my flashlight and shine it at the floor.

The gnome is broken in two. His head has come off his body. I pick up the two pieces. I take them to the back door and throw them as far away from the house as I can.

I go back to bed.

The nightmare is over.

"Are there any stories about mechanical gnomes in this book?" it said

The next morning I get up and go to the kitchen.

"There'd better not be." whispered the mechanical bird.

Grandpa is sitting at the kitchen table with his back to me.

"Morning, Grandpa," I call.

"Good morning, Andy," he says. "I found your friend in the backyard."

"Huh?" I say.

Grandpa turns around.

In his hand is the gnome. He has glued the head back onto the body.

A huge jagged crack runs from shoulder to shoulder. He looks even uglier than before.

"Gee, thanks, Grandpa."

"That's alright, son," he says. "Had an accident, did ya?"

"Uh, yeah, you could say that."

"You must be really attached to that gnome," says Grandpa, "to bring him all this way."

"Uh, yeah, you could say that, too," I say.

ELECTED BY A QUIRK OF THE ELECTORAL SYSTEM, The new Prime Minister BACK-GARDEN GNOME prepares to meet the press.

It's late afternoon. Grandma and Grandpa have gone out. I'm home alone. This is the moment I've been waiting for.

I pick up the gnome by his hat, hold him at arm's length and take him out to the backyard.

I've got a little job for Grandpa's mulcher.

I flick the switch. The engine roars. The mulcher is hungry — ready for action.

I pause.

More tree limbs.

What am I doing?! I am about to throw a garden gnome into a garden mulcher. The gnome is not smiling now. He's looking up at me with big pleading eyes like an innocent child. But this is just part of his evil magic. He is not a child. And he is definitely not innocent.

I push him into the mulcher.

He flies straight back out. The gnome is lying on the ground grinning at me. His two painted eyes are cold and black.

There is no doubt. The gnome is a killer. It's either him or me. I pick him up again.

"Say your prayers," I tell him.

I drop him into the top and use a tree branch to force him into the blades.

The blades whine. Or is that the gnome screaming?

The mulcher coughs out an enormous wad of dust and propels colored shrapnel into the air.

I flick the switch off.

All is silent.

I lean on the mulcher. Panting. Waiting. Half expecting the gnome dust to reassemble itself and come at me.

But nothing happens.

I have saved the world from the evil gnome. Not that anybody will ever know. I hate that. You do this brave heroic thing, and you can't tell anybody because if you do they'll think you're crazy.

I feel strangely out of place

I go back inside.

Grandma and Grandpa are home.

"Are you feeling alright?" asks Granny. "You look a little pale."

I'm a fly

47

OCCASIONAL
GARDEN
VISITORS
↓
EASTERN
BARRED
BANDICOOT

↓

SPINY
AUNT
EATER

↓

GLUE
TONGUED
LIZARD.

"I'm okay," I say. "Just a little tired. I'm going to lie down."

I push open the door of my bedroom.

I scream.

The gnome is lying on top of the bed. Staring straight at me. Grinning. He *has* reassembled himself. Payback time. The room starts spinning, and I fall to the floor.

Grandma and Grandpa rush in.

"Andy!" says Granny. "What's the matter?"

I'm trying to tell them, but nothing is coming out. I just open and shut my mouth like a fish out of water. I point to the gnome. My hand is shaking.

"The gnome," I whisper. "The gnome . . ."

"Do you like it?" says Grandpa, helping me up. "We found it at the market. It's exactly the same as your other one, only without a broken neck. Thought it might cheer you up."

"It's not the same gnome?"

"No, of course not," says Granny. "But it's almost identical. We thought you'd like it."

"I do! I do!" I say. "I love it!"

I pick it up, cuddle it, and give it a big kiss.

Grandma and Grandpa smile, pleased with their work. They leave.

I place the gnome back on the bed. I'm not

taking my eyes off him for a moment. But nothing happens.

I kneel down and put my face close to his.

"Any funny stuff and it's Grandpa's mulcher . . . just like your friend. Got it?"

The gnome just stares.

And smiles.

Well, it could be a smile. It could be a grimace. It's hard to tell.

INTERESTING GARDEN SCULPTURES.

49

Imaginary friends

A drawing by my friend the Imaginary Illustrator.

Tomorrow is our school field day. I don't want to go. Not because I'm not good at sports. I can run faster, jump higher, and throw stuff farther than anybody in the school, but I don't like to do it. It would be boring with me just winning everything all day long. I like to give the other kids a chance. That's just the sort of thoughtful person I am.

But try telling that to my Mom. She has this crazy idea that I don't like sports and that I try to get out of them whenever I can.

That's why I've brought Fred home. Fred's my imaginary friend. I'm going to tell Mom he's sick and that I have to stay home from school to look after him. It can't fail. Either she'll think I'm going crazy and keep me home from school, or she'll be sucked in and let me stay home to look after Fred. I can't lose.

I open the back door and drop my bag on the laundry room floor.

"Mom?" I call.

"I'm in here," she says.

I find her in the kitchen. She's chopping onions.

"Mom, I'd like you to meet a friend of mine. His name is Fred."

"But there's nobody there," says Mom.

"Don't be like that," I say. "You'll hurt his feelings."

Mom frowns.

"Are you feeling alright?"

"Who are you asking," I say. "Me or Fred?"

"You," she says.

"I'm fine," I say. "It's Fred who is not feeling so good. He's got a stomachache. He wants to know if I can stay home from school tomorrow to look after him."

I pretend to help Fred over to a chair. I go to the sink, run a sponge under cold water,

FAMOUS PAINTINGS # 12.

LEONAROO DA CHICKEN'S MONA LISA.

G'day Hello **51**

and then mop Fred's brow with it. Mom is watching me with a frown.

"I think he's running a temperature," I explain. "I don't want to miss out on field day, but I really think I should stay home and look after him."

"What about his parents?" says Mom.

"They've gone on a vacation overseas."

"And left him all alone?"

"They didn't want him to miss any school."

"I could look after him," says Mom.

"Don't be silly, Mom. You've got plenty to do without having to look after Fred as well."

"No, it would be a pleasure," says Mom. "Your friends are very important to me."

"Fred is very important to me, too," I say. "I wouldn't feel right leaving him."

"But I know how much field day means to you," says Mom.

"Yes, but I couldn't enjoy the day knowing Fred is home sick. If he gets any worse overnight, I'll have to stay home."

"I really don't think that will be necessary," says Mom. "I *am* a trained nurse. I think the best thing you could do for Fred would be to go out there tomorrow and just do your best. Make him proud of you."

Gee, I wish I could find a girlfriend with interesting ears.

(This picture should be on Pg 242)

"Maybe," I say. "Assuming that he lives long enough to hear the results."

"Dinner's ready," calls Mom.

I walk into the kitchen.

Mom has set three places. But there's only two of us. Jen is away on a school trip and Dad is on a work trip.

"Who's coming to dinner, Mom?"

She gives me a strange look.

"Why, Fred of course."

"Oh, yeah," I say. "Of course."

"Well," says Mom. "Don't just make him stand there. Invite him to sit down."

"Have a seat, Fred," I say.

Mom motions to me to pull the chair out for him.

We both know this is completely stupid, but to not do it would be to admit that Fred is not real. And that means field day for sure.

I walk around to the chair against the wall. I pull it out and bow low.

"Your chair, Monsieur Fred," I say.

I give him time to sit down and then I push his chair in.

Politician with Integrity by Hans. R. Loos.

A shadow of its former self.

Who's me?

I am me.

53

He'll never find me attractive with this tongue sticking out of my **ear**!

(This joke should be on page 242)

I just love imaginary Brussels sprouts.

Mom places a heaping plate of steaming casserole in front of Fred.

"There you are," she says. "I know you're probably not hungry, but try to eat as much as you can. You need to keep up your strength when you're as sick as you are."

My mouth is watering. I'm so hungry.

Mom places a plate in front of me. But it's not as generous as Fred's serving. In fact, it's hardly enough for a mouse.

"Is there a food shortage?" I say.

"There is tonight," she says, "I didn't plan for an extra guest. You'll have to share your dinner with Fred."

"But he's getting more than me."

"He's sick! Don't you want him to get better?"

"Well, of course I do, but . . ."

"But what?"

"It's no use for him to get better if I starve to death."

"Andy," says Mom. "I must say I'm a little shocked at your selfishness. Fred is a very sick boy. We have to do everything we can to help him."

"Yes, Mom."

I eat my dinner in about three seconds flat.

You are me?

No. No.

54

Fred, of course, doesn't touch his.

At the end of the meal, Mom starts collecting the plates.

"What's going to happen to Fred's dinner?" I say.

"I'll put it in the fridge. He might want it tomorrow."

"And if he doesn't want it, can I have it?"

"No, I don't think that would be a good idea," says Mom. "It's probably got his germs all over it. I don't want you getting sick as well."

Mom picks up his plate and stretches a sheet of Glad Wrap across it.

"Well," she says, "what are you waiting for? Go and set up the camping bed for Fred. I expect he'll be having an early night, poor thing."

"Can't he sleep in Jen's room?"

"But he's *your* friend. Besides, I think someone should be with him. In case he gets sick during the night."

I go to the hall closet to get the bed. I have to unpack about a billion other pieces of junk to get to it. Old surfboards, Dad's golf bag, a badminton set, boxes of Christmas decorations, and a huge red cooler have to be removed before I can reach the bed.

I drag it out. Looks like it was the first-ever camping bed—made before they'd figured out how to make them properly. It weighs about seventeen tons. Its springs are all sticking out at crazy angles. I lug the beast down the hallway. One of the springs catches on my windbreaker. I start to undo it. A daddy long-legs appears from the top of the mattress. It's right in front of my eyes. I get so scared that I knock over the bed. It falls onto my foot. A perfect five-toe crush.

"FRUIT TINGLES!" I scream.

"Andy!" says Mom from the living room. "Language! We have a guest, remember?"

How could I forget? I've got five toes' worth of throbbing pain to remind me.

THE CAMP BED STRIKES BACK.

I drag the camping bed the rest of the way up the hall and into my bedroom. I wrestle with the latch. The bed springs open with lethal force.

I go to the linen closet and get sheets, blankets, and a pillow.

I bring them back and start making the bed. If there's one thing I hate, it's making beds. I can never get them smooth. There's always this stupid ripple running from one cor-

But you can't be me

56

ner to the other. Someone should invent spray-on sheets. They would make a fortune.

After about five hours I finish the bed. I come back to the living room.

Tonight it's *The Simpsons*. I've been looking forward to watching it all day. But Mom is watching some stupid documentary about the economy.

"Mom, can we watch *The Simpsons*?"

"Well, I wouldn't mind," she says, "but Fred said he prefers documentaries. . . . He's very intellectual, you know."

"Very funny, Mom," I say. This has gone far enough. I don't care about field day any more. I just want to watch *The Simpsons*.

"I surrender," I say. "You win, okay?"

"What do you mean?" asks Mom.

"There's no such person as Fred!"

"Andy," says Mom. "You'll hurt Fred's feelings."

"But he doesn't have any feelings. He doesn't exist!"

"Andy, that is a horrible thing to say. How would you like it if Fred said you didn't exist?"

"That would be a laugh. Somebody who

Hi, I'm JUST ANNOYING.

The new Prime Minister, Mr Camp Bed, speaks to the public.

Why not?

57

doesn't exist telling somebody who does exist that they don't exist."

"That's it. Fred and I have had enough of your rudeness. Go to your room."

I'm home from the school field day. I can hardly walk. My legs are aching. And I didn't win a single ribbon. Not that I tried, of course. I had to let the others have a shot.

The house is empty. The lights are off. Mom is out.

I'm in the kitchen spooning honey over a bowl of Cheerios when the front door opens.

I can hear Mom talking and laughing.

She comes into the kitchen. She is holding a stick of cotton candy.

"Where have you been?" I ask.

"At the zoo," she says.

"Why didn't you take me?"

"Well, I know how much field day means to you. Besides, I wanted to do something special for Fred."

I pound my fist on the table. "Fred's my imaginary friend," I yell, "not yours. You've got no right to take him to the zoo without me."

"Come now, Andy," says Mom. "Fred's had

58

a pretty miserable time of it. We have to make allowances."

I look at the fresh stick of cotton candy in her hand. Pink, shiny, and fluffy. Perfect.

"Is that for me?" I ask.

"No," says Mom. "It's Fred's."

"Can I have some?"

"Well, I don't know. You'll have to ask Fred."

I feel really dumb asking an imaginary person for cotton candy, but I'm desperate. Mom never buys cotton candy for me.

"Fred," I say to the blank space where Fred is supposed to be standing, "may I please have some of your cotton candy?"

We both look at the blank space.

I can't hear anything, but Mom is nodding intently.

She turns to me.

"He says he'd prefer not to share it with you because he's worried that you'll get his disease."

"It's not fair. Why does Fred get cotton candy and I don't?"

"Because it rots your teeth."

"What about Fred's teeth?" I say.

"He's sick. Surely you wouldn't begrudge him this little pleasure, would you?"

Mr. Scribble and his angry wife.

Mrs CAMP BED COMPETES IN THE SKI JUMP AT THE WINTER OLYMPICS. (Unsuccessfully, she folded after the first round)

We must be related.

I give up. I might as well try bashing down a brick wall with my head. Mom's not going to budge.

"Andy," says Mom, "would you mind sleeping on the camping bed tonight? Fred's had such a big day at the zoo. I think he needs the comfort of a real bed. Would you mind? Please? He is our guest."

"Yeah, right, Mom," I say. "And would you like me to sit by his bed and hold a bucket for him to throw up all his cotton candy into as well?"

Mom looks shocked.

"There's no need to talk like that, Andy."

"Get it into your head, Mom — there is no Fred!"

"I'm sorry, Andy," says Mom, "but this is no way to treat a guest. Please go to your room right now, and don't come out until you can be civil."

I go to my room. I would stomp except my legs are aching and my crushed toes are still hurting. I have to do a sort of angry limp instead.

I wish I'd never invented Fred. He's stolen my dinner, my television show, my trip to the zoo — and even my mother. And now he

The WORLD'S BEST ANNOYING TRICK.

⌐ᴸᴸᴵ¹⌐ᴵᴼ
I -- ᴼᴸᴵᴵᴵ-I
I-ᴼᴸᴵ¹¹ᴸᴵ
ᴸ¹-ᴸᴵ-¹⌐ᴼ

We apologize that this trick appears in code.

For the translation see Pg 22 of GRIFFITH'S MAMMOTH ANNOYING TRICK CODE BOOK Vol.4 (Available at all good BOOKSTORES).

You don't even exist.

60

wants my bed. Well, forget it. Fred has to go. There's not enough room in the house for the both of us.

But how do you get rid of someone who doesn't exist in the first place?

I've got it. You invent somebody else who doesn't exist to get rid of them for you.

I need an imaginary friend who's not going to turn out to be a mama's boy like Fred. He's got to be bad. Superbad. His name is going to be Damien. He doesn't wash his hands after going to the bathroom. He doesn't say please, and he doesn't say thank you. He wears his baseball cap backward and goes swimming less than half an hour after big meals. He sticks forks in toasters just for the fun of it. He doesn't talk about his problems — he solves them with violence, and plenty of it. He hates vegetables. He hates girls. And, most of all, he hates goody-goodies. And tomorrow I will introduce him to Fred.

I'm woken by the sound of Mom's laughter.

I put my bathrobe on over my pajamas and go to the door of the kitchen.

Mom is fussing around Fred's chair.

She sees me standing at the door.

"Good morning, Andy," she says. "Come in and join us."

"Mom," I say. "I'd like you to meet another friend of mine. His name is Damien. His parents are overseas."

Mom doesn't miss a beat. She comes across to me and mimes a handshake with Damien.

"Pleased to meet you, Damien," she says. "Would you like some breakfast?"

"Is that alright, Mom?" I ask. "I know it's kind of short notice, but . . ."

"Shush, Andy," says Mom. "Damien's talking."

"Sorry," I say.

Mom stands listening to Damien. She laughs.

"Have a seat," says Mom, pulling out a chair for Damien. "Would you like some oatmeal?"

"Yes," I say. "I'm starving."

Mom glares at me.

"I was talking to Damien."

She takes his order.

"What a lovely boy," she says to me as she crosses to the stove. "And so polite."

Damien? Polite? But he's not supposed to say please or thank you. And he's supposed to

SUN TAN
FOR RATS.

ANSWER TO
SPOT THE
DIFFERENCE
Pg 12.

It's a
trick.

A   B

The pictures
are the
same. In B
the universe
was rotated
through 180°

- TV
- STAR -

I
can't
see
you.

hate girls. That includes mothers. What's wrong with me? Am I losing my touch? Am I going soft? Is it really so hard to invent an imaginary friend that my mother won't fall in love with?

"Mom, what about me?" I say. "Can I have some oatmeal?"

"There's not much oatmeal left," she says. "But there's a little bit of toast . . . if you don't mind the crusts, that is. Fred doesn't like the crusts, so I gave him the rest of the loaf. I hope you don't mind."

I look at Fred's plate piled high with freshly buttered toast. There's at least ten pieces there.

Mom places two blackened, shriveled crusts in front of me.

"They got a little burnt," she says. "And I'm afraid there's no butter left, either."

"Don't tell me," I say. "You used it all on Fred's toast."

"That's right," says Mom. "How did you know?"

"Just a hunch," I say.

The telephone rings. Mom goes into the living room to answer it. Now is my chance.

WOULD YOU RATHER...
ANSWER from Pg 83.

B was/is the correct answer. 9 out of 10 young adults prefer to wear a pickaxe through their nostrils than any other body part.

It's cool and its unambiguous.

It's you that doesn't exist.

Mr
Scribble.
How
Cool
is he?

WIN A
FREE
GARDEN
GNOME
Answer
this simple
quiz
question:

If two trains
were
traveling
in opposite
directions
on separate
tracks 5km
apart..They
both leave
the same
station...
(Question
continues
Pg 98)

I sit down in Fred's chair and help myself to his toast.

Mom comes in. She flips.

"Andy! What are you doing? That's Fred's breakfast."

"He had to go," I say. "Damien, too."

Mom looks at Damien's chair and then back to mine.

"But I didn't get to say good-bye."

"I know," I say. "They slipped out while you were on the phone."

"But why?"

I have to think fast.

"Their parents came home early. They said to say thanks and all that. They would have said good-bye themselves but they didn't want to disturb you."

Mom sits down, shaking her head.

"But I was going to cook Fred's favorite dinner tonight. Cauliflower surprise. He told me he'd be here."

"Oh, well," I say, "Fred's like that. Damien, too. Nice boys, but very unreliable. When it comes down to it, they're both just out for themselves."

Mom looks like she's about to cry. This is going too far. Dad and Jen have obviously

But
I'm
ME!!

been away too long. I have to snap her out of it. Tell her the truth.

"Listen, Mom," I say. "There's something you have to understand. Fred and Damien were not real. I made them up."

"You did?"

"Yes," I say. "But I never counted on you getting so attached to them."

Mom doesn't say anything.

She stares at the table.

I feel like I've just committed a double homicide.

But I think I've finally gotten through. Sometimes the truth hurts.

I get up and pull out a chair next to hers.

"It's okay, Mom," I say. "You've still got me. *I'm* real." I go to sit down.

Mom screams.

"You can't sit there," she says. "It's taken."

I sigh.

"Mom, I thought we'd gotten this straight. There is no Fred. There is no Damien. There's just you and me."

"And Frieda," says Mom nodding toward the empty chair.

"Frieda?"

"Yes," says Mom. "She'll be staying with

Mrs Smith and her dining room table vacationing on the Gold Coast.

I feel so empty

No! I'm me.

65

CAULIFLOWER
SURPRISE

us for a few weeks. See, her parents have gone overseas and . . ."

"Don't tell me, Mom," I say. "She hates crusts."

"That's right," says Mom.

"And her favorite meal is cauliflower surprise?"

"Right again," says Mom, beaming. "How did you know?"

"Just a hunch," I say.

You've just Annoying.

SLURP!!!

In the shower
with Andy

I'm in the shower. Singing. And not just because the echo makes my voice sound so cool either. I'm singing because I'm so happy.

Ever since I've been old enough to take showers, I've been trying to find a way to fill a shower stall up with water. If I put a washcloth over the drain I can get the water as far up as my ankles, but it always ends up leaking out through the gaps in the door.

But I think I've finally found the answer — Dad's caulk gun.

I've plugged up the drain.

I've sealed up the shower doors.

I've filled in all the cracks in the tiles.

In the making of this story no face washers were harmed.

MR. SILICONE

The shower stall is completely watertight and the water is already up to my knees.

And the best thing is that I've got all night to enjoy it.

Even the humblest bar of soap can dream of greatness.

Mom and Dad have Mr. and Mrs. Bainbridge over for dinner. They'll be too busy listening to Mr. Bainbridge talking about himself to have time to worry about what I'm doing.

I hear banging on the door.

"Have you almost finished, Andy?"

It's Jen!

"No," I say. "I think I'm going to be in here a while yet."

"Can you hurry up?" yells Jen.

"But you already had your shower this morning," I yell.

"I'm going out," she says. "I need the bathroom!"

"Okay. I'll be out in a minute," I call. I always say that. It's the truth. Sort of. I will be out in a minute — I'm just not saying which minute it will be.

The shower stall is filling with thick white steam. Just the way I like it. Dad's always telling us how important it is to turn the fan on when we're taking a shower, but I don't see the point. A shower without steam doesn't make sense. You might as well go stand outside in the rain.

My rubber duck bumps against my legs. I pick it up.

"This is it," I say. "Just you and me . . . going where no boy — or rubber duck — has ever gone before."

It has its bill raised in a sort of a smile. It must be as excited as I am. Let's face it, there can't be that much excitement in the life of a rubber duck. Except that you'd get to see everybody without their clothes on.

Jen bangs on the door again.

"Andy! Pleeeeease!"

"Okay," I call. "I'll be out in a minute."

"You said that a minute ago."

"I'm washing my hair."

"But you've been in there for at least half an hour. You don't have *that* much hair."

"I'm using a new sort of shampoo — I have to do it strand by strand."

"Andy!"

The water is almost up to my belly button. There's only one thing missing. Bubbles!

I pick up the bubblebath and measure out a capful. I tip it into the water. A few bubbles,

NEW FROM
20th CENTURY
FLOPS
A
MOVIE
WITH
A
DIFFERENCE
BRANDO!
The
NASTY
RUBBER
DUCKY

He chews
ankles,
terrorizes
face washers,
pulls out
bath plugs...
BATH
TIME
WILL
NEVER
BE
THE
SAME.

but not enough. I add another cap. And another. And another. One more for good measure. Another for good luck.

I keep adding bubblebath until the bottle is empty. The bubbles rise over my head. Cool. It's like I'm being eaten by this enormous white fungus. Well, not that being eaten by an enormous white fungus would be cool — it would probably be quite uncool, actually — but you know what I mean.

Jen is yelling. "Andy, if you don't get out right this minute, you're going to be sorry."

Jen is persistent, I'll give her that. But I'll fix her. I'll use my old "what did you say?" routine.

"Pardon?" I yell. "What did you say?"

"I said you're going to be sorry."

"What? I can't hear you!"

"I said get out of the shower!"

"Pardon?"

No reply. I win.

Aaaaagghhh!

The water's gone hot! Boiling hot!

Jen must have flushed the toilet. That's bad news.

I lose.

I jump back against the shower wall.

Hot water splatters onto my face. My chest. My arms.

I grab the cold tap and turn it on full.

The hot water disappears. Now it's freezing.

I'm going to have to turn both taps off and start all over again. I hate that. Being a pioneer is not easy.

BATHROOM DANGERS NO 37

BATH SHARKS.

I turn the hot tap off. But the cold won't budge.

I grab the tap with both hands. I try to twist it clockwise but it's stuck. Not even my superstrength can move it.

The caulk gun is hanging off the shower pipe. I pick it up and start bashing the tap with it. That should loosen it.

But the handgrip shatters.

The pieces disappear into the soapy water. I'm staring at a thin metal rod coming out of the wall. And the water is still flowing full blast.

Help! It's BRANDO!

THE NASTY RUBBER DUCK.

I kneel down and clamp my teeth over the tap rod.

No good. The tap feels like it's rusted into place. My teeth will crack before it moves.

There's no steam left. The bubbles have

Hello little green men.

been flattened. The freezing water is almost up to my chest. Maybe this wasn't such a great idea.

Time to bail out.

I take a deep breath and dive to the bottom of the shower. I'm trying to find the drain. I've got to get the caulk out before the shower fills up completely.

But I can't do it. I did the job too well. There's nothing but a hard rubbery slab of caulk where the drain used to be. I can't poke through it. I can't get a fingernail underneath to lift it up. It's times like this I wish I didn't bite my nails. But then it's times like this that cause me to bite my nails in the first place.

I stand up, gasping for air. The water is up to my neck. I grab hold of the door handle and try to wrench it open but I laid the caulk even thicker on the doors than the drain. If you ever want anything sealed tight I can recommend Dad's caulk gun. This stuff stays stuck forever.

I'm going to have to break the door down.

I'll use the gun. It made short work of the tap, so the door shouldn't be a problem.

I bash the glass with the gun handle. It bounces off. I bash it again, harder this time.

SHOWER STALL WILDLIFE GUIDE:

DUCK BRUSH

WASHER FISH

LEGO CRUSTACEAN

TOE-NAIL CLIPPING

BELLY-BUTTON FLUFF

SOAP SLIVER

DRAIN KELP.

The gun snaps in two. Just my luck. Reinforced shower door glass. Unbreakable.

I'm shivering. And not just from the cold. I'm scared.

I start bashing the door with the duck.

"HELP! I'M DROWNING! HELP!"

"I'm not surprised!" Jen yells back. "You've been in there long enough."

"Jen, I'm not kidding. Help me!"

"What did you say?" she says. "I can't hear you."

"Be serious," I yell. "I've caulked myself in here."

"What?"

She wins again.

I'm treading water. My head is very close to the top of the shower.

The only way I can save myself is to get rid of the water.

I'm going to have to drink it.

Dirty soapy shower water.

I'd rather die.

The water nudges the tip of my nose.

Actually, on second thought, I'd rather drink the water.

I start swallowing.

It's working. I just have to drink as fast as

WIN FABULOUS PRIZES!! continued from Pg 37 ... send it to: The Chicken Marketing BOARD P.O Box 100,000,000 in your capital city. If you have the number right, you will receive ABSOLUTELY FREE... A... see Pg 89 or Pg 41 or Pg 115

BATHROOM DANGERS.

INNOCENT LOOKING DARK HAIRS STICKING OUT OF DRAIN.
BE CAREFUL, THERE IS A COMPLETE LIFE FORM ATTACHED

HAIR

SOAP GLOB

LEGO

GOLF BALL

FALSE TEETH

Mr. Scribble !!!

TOOTH BRUSH

BABY'S PACIFIER.

SPUNK!

the shower is filling up. And if I can drink even faster, then I might get out of here alive yet. Actually the water doesn't taste that bad — it's only been three days since my last shower.

I keep swallowing.

And swallowing. And swallowing. And swallowing.

Uh-oh.

I can't believe this.

I need to go to the bathroom.

But I can't.

I'll drink dirty shower water but I won't drink that.

I've got to hold on.

But I can't do that either.

I'm busting.

My head is bumping against the roof of the shower.

It's getting harder to breathe.

There's more banging on the door but it sounds like it's coming from a long way away.

"I'm going to tell Dad," says Jen in a distant voice. "Is that what you want? Is it?"

"Yes Jen," I call. "Yes! Please hurry!"

74

Everything becomes quiet.

My life is flashing before my eyes.

I see myself blowing a high-pitched whistle while Mom is trying to talk on the telephone. I see myself letting air out of the tires on Dad's car. I see myself hiding a rubber snake in Jen's bed. Is that all I did with my life? Annoy people? Surely I did something useful. . . . Something good?

Nope. I can't think of anything. Except for solving the problem of how to fill a shower stall with water.

I may be going to die, but at least it will be a hero's death. Future generations of Australian children will thank me as they float around in their sealed-up shower stalls.

Ouch!

Something is pressing into the top of my head.

I look up.

The fan! I forgot all about it.

It's not very big, but it's better than nothing. If I can get the grille off, then I can escape through the hole and up into the roof.

I work my fingers under the edge of the grille and pull on it. It comes off easily.

I reach into the casing and grab hold of

75

the fan. I rock it back and forth. There is a little bit of give in it. I start giving it all I've got.

Finally the bolts holding it give way. I push my arms and head into the hole, kicking like mad to get the boost I need to make it all the way up.

The opening is smaller than I thought. I expel every last bit of air in my lungs to make myself thin enough to fit through the hole. Not that there was much air left in them, but it seems to help.

At last! I'm through!

...And so the cricket is interrupted, once again, by a brief shower.

I'm lying on a yellow insulation patch above the ceiling of our house. The glass fibers are prickly on my skin, but I'm not complaining. It's a lot better than where I was. I look back into the hole. It's like one of those fishing holes that Eskimos cut in the ice. But there's no fish. Just my rubber duck. I reach down and pick it out. We're in this together. I can't just leave it.

After I get my breath back, I look around.

I know there's a manhole in the top of the kitchen. All I have to do is to locate it, climb down into the kitchen and sneak down the hallway into my room. Then I can put my pajamas on and go to bed early. It will save a

SPUNK!

munch munch

lot of boring explanations — and, if I'm really lucky, Jen will get the blame.

I have to move fast. I start crawling toward the kitchen. I'm carrying the duck in one hand and using my other hand to feel my way along the roof beam.

Suddenly I feel a sharp pain in my thumb. I jerk my hand back and almost lose my balance. I fling the duck away so I can grab the beam with my other hand.

I look at my thumb. A huge splinter is sticking out of it. I pull it out with my teeth. Ouch!

I shake my hand a few times and look around for my duck. It has landed in the middle of a large unsupported section of insulation. I'm tempted to leave it there. But that wouldn't be right. It's been with me all the way. I can't abandon it now.

I reach toward it but it's too far away. I'm going to have to crawl out there. I know you're not supposed to climb on the unsupported parts of the ceiling, but I think it will be okay. I'm not that heavy. And it's not as if I have any clothes on to weigh me down.

I climb carefully onto the unsupported section and start moving slowly to the center. One more foot and I'm there.

I pick up my duck and bring it up to my face. "Just you and me," I say.

The duck creaks. That's weird. I didn't know rubber ducks could talk.

Uh-oh. The creaking is not coming from the duck. It's coming from underneath me. The ceiling is giving way.

I try to grab the wooden beam but I can't reach it.

The ceiling caves in.

Next thing I know, I'm lying, legs spread, in the middle of the dinner table — my fall broken by an insulation mat.

As the dust from the ceiling plaster settles, I see Mr. and Mrs. Bainbridge and Mom and Dad staring down at me.

Jen is standing next to Dad, her bath towel draped over her shoulder. Her back is turned toward me, and she's so busy complaining to Dad that she doesn't seem to notice what has happened.

". . . I've asked him a million times but he just won't get out . . ." she's saying.

"Oh, dear," says Mom.

"Oh, my," says Mrs. Bainbridge.

For once in his life, Mr. Bainbridge is speechless.

"Oh, no," says Dad, shaking his head at me. "No, no, no!"

"Oh, yes," says Jen. "And I'll tell you what else . . ."

Dad nods in my direction.

Jen stops, turns around, and stares.

I cover myself with the rubber duck, swing my legs over the edge of the table, and stand up.

"I beg your pardon," I say. "I was looking for the kitchen."

Nobody says anything. They are all just staring at me, their faces and clothes white from the plaster dust.

I head toward the door as fast as I can.

As I'm about to exit, I turn toward Jen. She is still standing there, eyes wide.

"Well, what are you waiting for?" I say. "Shower's free!"

**Would you rather? Would you rather?
Would you rather? Would you rather?
Would you rather? Would you rather?
Would you rather? Would you rather?**

I f you had the choice, Dad," I say, "would you rather be eaten by ants or lions?"

"It depends," he says. He's holding the ketchup bottle up to his eye and peering into the neck of it like it's a telescope.

"Blast!" he says. "It's blocked again!"

"Language!" says Mom.

"'Blast' is not a swear word," says Dad.

"It's not a nice word," says Mom.

I'd rather be fricasseed in bagel crumbs and served in a white wine sauce to wealthy industrialists.

"Well?" I say. "Ants or lions?"

Dad puts the bottle down. He rubs his chin with his hand and frowns. "I can't say I'm too keen on being eaten by either," he says. "Can I have an injection to put me to sleep beforehand?"

"No. You have to be conscious."

"Hmmm. In that case, I'll take the lions. If I have to experience pain, I'd rather it be short and sharp. Ants would take too long."

"What if the lions were really old, though," I say. "And their teeth were all falling out and they just gummed you to death and it took ages and ages and ages?"

"Do we have to talk about this while we're eating?" says Jen.

"It's important," I say. "You might be in the situation where you have to choose one day. You'll be a lot better off if you've already thought about it."

"Yeah, right," says Jen, rolling her eyes.

Dad is holding the ketchup bottle at a forty-five degree angle and poking his steak knife into its neck.

"You'll cut yourself if you're not careful," says Mom.

"I'll be careful," says Dad.

"Dad?" I say, trying to get him back on the topic. I wish Jen and Mom wouldn't interrupt. Dad gets distracted so easily.

"Owww!" Dad slams the bottle down and drops the knife. He's shaking his left hand and grimacing.

"What happened?" says Mom.

WOULD YOU RATHER BE SPLIT IN TWO ↑VERTICALLY

OR ↑HORIZONTALLY

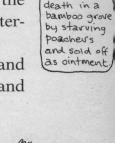

I'd rather be beaten to death in a bamboo grove by starving poachers and sold off as ointment.

what?

81

Anyway... What makes you think I'd want to eat him!!?

"The knife slipped," he says.

"I told you to be careful. Use the barbecue sauce instead."

"I don't want barbecue sauce," says Dad. "There's plenty of ketchup — I just can't get it out!"

"Forget the ketchup," I say. "Ants or lions?"

"I told you," he says. "I'll take the lions, but I want good ones. Really hungry, really mean, and really quick. One swipe and lights out. No gumming!"

"You can't make demands. You have to take what you get."

Speaking on behalf of the ants, we'd rather eat the mother.

"Then I don't want to sign up."

"You're already signed up!" I say. "It's ants or lions. If you don't want lions then you must want ants."

"No," says Dad. "Ants are out of the question." He turns the ketchup bottle upside down and stands it on his plate.

"That will tip over," says Mom.

"I'm watching it," says Dad.

"That's what I'm worried about," says Mom.

"What's wrong with ants?" I ask.

"Two slow."

"What if your body was covered in honey to attract as many ants as possible?"

"Well, honey would attract sugar ants, and I wouldn't mind that so much," says Dad. "They'd just eat the honey and leave me alone."

"They'd be all over you, though."

"But they'd be after the honey, not me."

"No honey then. You'll be covered in dog food instead," I say.

"Charming!" says Jen. "Could you pass the salt, Andy?"

"Say please."

"Please."

"Pretty please."

"Pretty please," she sighs.

Jen says it because she knows it's quicker to say it than to argue with me about saying it.

"Pretty please with sugar on top," I say.

"Andy! Just pass the freakin' salt!"

"Jen!" says Mom. "Language!"

"Well, he wouldn't pass the freakin' salt."

"There's still no need to speak like that."

Jen looks at me through slitted eyes.

I slide the salt shaker across the table.

"Here you go Jen," I say.

"Thank you."

"Don't mention it. You're welcome. Any time. If there's anything else you require, please don't hesitate to let me know."

WOULD
YOU
RATHER...
have a
pickaxe
inserted
in the

A: top of
your nose?

or

B: fleshy
division
betwixt
your
nostrils?

For correct
answer see
Pg 63.

83

"There is something else," she says.

"Anything," I say.

"Shut up!"

"Jen!" says Mom.

Jen sticks her tongue out at me.

I ignore her and turn to Dad. "Well? How about it — would you consider the dog food?"

"But I don't want to be covered in dog food!" says Dad. "If I have to die, I at least want a little dignity."

"But I thought you wanted to die quickly," I say.

"I do. I'll stick with the lions."

"What if by covering yourself in dog food I could guarantee you that the ants would finish you off ten times quicker than even the most efficient lions?"

"Now you're just being silly," says Dad in a loud voice. He's getting heated up. "You're making promises that you can't keep. I've seen lions. I've seen their claws."

He curls up the fingers on his right hand to demonstrate a lion's claw.

"One swipe can break your neck."

He swipes his arm across the table so that his "claw" goes within a centimeter of my nose.

The ketchup bottle goes flying. It clatters

84

across the kitchen floor. It comes to rest next to the fridge, spinning slowly.

"I told you that would happen," says Mom.

But Dad ignores her. "Are you trying to tell me that ants would be able to kill me faster?"

"You're assuming that the lions will have claws," I say.

And some chips for the cubs.

"Well what *do* they have? No teeth, no claws? Are they blind, deaf, and paralyzed as well? Why don't I just eat myself and save them the trouble?"

"Now you're the one being silly," I say. "Eating yourself is not an option. It's ants or lions."

Dad shakes his head. He gets up from the table and picks up the ketchup bottle.

Jen screws up her face.

"These mashed potatoes taste funny," she says.

"What's wrong with them?" says Mom.

"They're sweet."

Jen picks up the salt shaker. She examines it closely.

"Does this salt look right to you?" says Jen.

"Pass it over here," says Mom. She holds the shaker up to the light. "It's sugar," she says.

"Andy!" says Jen.

"Yes, Jen?" I say innocently.

Go AWAY, stupid thing!

Why do big brothers/ sisters automatically blame their little sisters/ brothers for everything?

A. Because the brats did it.

B. It makes them feel better.

C. They love watching little kids being punished.

D. A, B, and C.

"Did you do that?"

"Do what?"

"You know very well what."

"What?"

"Fill the salt shaker with sugar!"

"No," I say. It's not a lie, either. I only half-filled it.

Mom sighs. "Go and get another serving," she says. "There's plenty more in the pot."

"That's not the point," says Jen. "He should be punished. Dad, Andy filled the salt shaker with sugar and now my dinner's wrecked."

"And there's no chance to escape?" says Dad.

"Huh?" says Jen.

"I'm talking to Andy," he says.

"No," I say. "There's no escape. None at all."

I stick my tongue out at Jen. Dad is more interested in my hypothetical than in her whining.

ANTS CAN BE VERY SNEAKY.

"Well, that's not very fair," says Dad. "People don't want to go see helpless people being eaten by ants and lions week in, week out."

"I would," says Jen. "Especially if it was Andy being eaten."

"Nonsense!" says Dad. "You'd get bored.

You don't scare me.

86

You wouldn't want to go to the game to see Carlton thrash Collingwood every week, even if you were a Carlton supporter. You need to give the underdog a chance to keep it interesting."

"Maybe," I say, "but you're assuming it's a public event."

"It's not?" says Dad.

"No. Nobody's watching. It's just you and the lions. Or the ants."

Dad looks puzzled.

"Then what's the point?"

"I don't know," I say, "but it doesn't matter. The point is to answer the question."

"I've answered your question," he says. "I said I would rather the lions."

"Is that your final answer?" I say.

"Yes, as long as they're efficient, I'll take the lions."

"That's not an answer — there's no guarantee."

Dad picks up the ketchup bottle again, turns it upside down, and starts slapping the bottom with the palm of his hand. A couple of red drops splatter onto the plate and the tablecloth.

"You'll end up with ketchup all over yourself if you don't watch out," says Mom.

WOULD YOU RATHER?

Would you rather be a
+ PIMPLE
or a
+ BOIL?

WRITE YOUR ANSWER IN 50 WORDS OR LESS AND SEND TO THE MANAGER, STATUE OF LIBERTY, New York, USA.

LIONS

GO LIONS

EEEK!

87

This meal is still frozen in the middle.

I am the QUEEN of ORSTRALIA!

I insist that you allow me to be eaten alive by a brace of babbling barred bandicoots.

MOTHER, that sounds fabulous. Count me in, too.

"Jen?" I say.

Jen shoots me a mean look. "If you're going to ask me whether I'd rather be eaten by ants or lions then forget it."

"I'm not going to ask you whether you'd rather be eaten by ants or lions."

"Promise?"

"Cross my heart, hope to die, stick a needle in my eye."

"Okay, what?"

"Would you rather be eaten by lions or ants?"

Jen points her fork at me. "You just broke your promise."

"No, I didn't."

"Yes, you did. Now you have to stick a needle in your eye."

"No, I don't."

Jen gets up from the table.

"Where are you going?" says Dad.

"To get a needle," she says. Jen turns to me. "Would you rather a long sharp one or a short blunt one?"

"Nobody will be sticking needles in anybody's eye at this dinner table!" says Mom.

"But he broke his promise," says Jen.

Go away

"No, I didn't," I say. "I promised I wouldn't ask you if you'd rather be eaten by ants or lions."

"But you did," says Jen.

"I didn't. I asked you whether you would rather be eaten by *lions or ants*."

"Same thing!" says Jen.

"No, it isn't."

"Is so."

"Jen," I say. "Whether or not I broke my promise, and whether or not I would prefer a long sharp needle to a short blunt needle or a short blunt needle to a long sharp needle is irrelevant. The real question is whether you would rather be eaten by lions or ants."

"You broke your promise," she says. "And you made me pour sugar all over my dinner."

There's no point asking Jen. She's too bitter. And Dad is too interested in the ketchup bottle to give me a serious answer. That leaves only one person.

"What about you, Mom?" I say. "What would you rather?"

"Oh, I don't know."

"What don't you know?" I say. "It's a very

WIN
FABULOUS
PRIZES!!
Continued
from Pg 73
...A
FROZEN
CHICKEN
HAT.
Approved
of by the
BLUE SKY
PROTECTION
SOCIETY.
Frozen
chicken
hats
are
guaranteed
to prevent
90% of
BLUE SKY
RAYS
(very
harmful)
from
getting
to
your
face

89

simple question. What more do you need to know?"

"Well," she says. "Why is this happening to me? What have I done?"

"It doesn't matter!"

"I think it does. If I'm going to be eaten by ants or lions, I want to know why."

I love eating people. The only meal you can chat to while you eat.

"It's the choice that's important," I say.

"But how can I make a sensible choice if I don't know why I've been put there in the first place?" asks Mom. "Am I being punished, or have I just been picked at random?"

I sigh. Mom can be very stubborn.

"Okay," I say. "You're being punished."

"What for?"

"Mom!"

"Well, I need to know what I've done. That way I can decide whether the ants or the lions are the more appropriate punishment."

"But how does it change things?"

"Well, suppose I committed a whole lot of small crimes. I think the ants would be the best punishment. But if I did something really bad, something really big, then I think the lions would be the best."

"Okay," I say, "but suppose you did lots of

90

I'm the PAGE NUMBER fly

small crimes and a couple of really big ones as well. What then?"

"Then I think both ants and lions would be appropriate."

"No, you have to choose one."

"But I would deserve both."

"But which one would you prefer?"

"Prefer?" says Mom. "I don't like the idea of either option very much."

Here we go again.

"Cubs would be alright," she says thoughtfully.

"Huh?"

"Lion cubs. They would be nice. They're very playful."

"But they're still going to eat you."

"But they'd do it in a playful way."

That does it.

"I'm just asking a simple question!" I say, slamming my fist down on the table. "Would you rather be eaten by ants or by lions? Why can't anybody just answer the question?"

Everybody is quiet.

Everybody except for Dad. He's busy whacking the ketchup bottle like his life depends on getting ketchup right this minute.

Suddenly ketchup explodes from the bottle. It splurts onto his plate, the tablecloth, and his clothes. Down his shirt, onto his pants, and all over the floor.

He looks at Mom.

"Don't say anything!" he says.

"I wasn't going to," she says.

I can't help laughing.

"What's so funny?" says Dad, wiping ketchup out of his eye. "Did you have something to do with this?"

Of course I did. But I'm not about to admit it.

"It's not fair," I say. "Why do I get blamed for every little thing that goes wrong around here?"

"Because every little thing that goes wrong around here is your fault," says Jen. "Punish him, Dad. He gets away with everything."

"Andy," says Dad. "I'm going to ask you a question, and I want you to think very carefully about the answer. Tell me, would you rather lose your allowance for one week or do double chores for two weeks?"

"But you're assuming I'm guilty," I say.

"I'm not assuming you're guilty — I know it! Now, which would you rather?"

92

Uh-oh. This is not right. I'm supposed to be the one asking the questions.

"Dad, before I answer, tell me one thing."

"What's that?" he says.

"If you had to be squashed, would you rather be squashed by bricks or feathers?"

He frowns.

I'd rather be pecked to death by chickens

"Don't answer, Dad," says Jen. "He's just trying to distract you."

Dad ignores Jen.

"Probably feathers, I think," says Dad. "They're softer."

I'd rather be trampled to death by rhinos.

"But there will still be enough to squash you," I say. "Why not choose the bricks? They're not as soft, but they might be quicker."

"Hmmm," he says. "That depends. Would they be dropped all together or one at a time?"

I insist on having my brains sucked out by a giant AARDVARK.

Jen pushes her chair back loudly and stomps off from the table. I don't blame her. We could be here for quite a while.

Right now, please

CLUNK!

Phew

Murder, bloody murder!

"MURDER, BLOODY MURDER!"

I'm yelling at the top of my voice. So is Danny. I look at him. He looks at me. We nod. I take a deep breath.

"MURDER, BLOODY MURDER!" we shout.

Sooty joins in, barking and howling.

We wait. But nothing happens. Nobody comes. No police sirens. My neighbors don't even bother sticking their heads over the fence to see what the trouble is.

"It's no use," says Danny. "Nobody cares."

I kick a divot out of the lawn.

"It would be too bad if we were really getting murdered," I say. "I bet they'd be sorry then. Let's try one more time."

I would just like to say that I'm in the wrong story.

"Alright," says Danny. "Once more and then that's it. I've got a sore throat."

"MURDER!" we scream. "BLOODY MURDER!"

"Would you idiots shut up!" says Mr. Broadbent. "I'm trying to work."

Mr. Broadbent is standing in our driveway. Mr. Broadbent lives next door. He's a university lecturer. He works in a little room right next to our fence.

"How did you know that we weren't really being murdered?" I ask him.

"Because you've been calling out for the last half an hour," he says. "But, I swear, if you don't shut up, I'll come back and murder you myself. And your dog!"

Mr. Broadbent turns around and stomps back down the drive.

Sooty slinks off into his kennel. Danny and I look at each other. We don't say anything.

We're too scared.

Mr. Broadbent has just threatened to murder us.

"Did you hear that?" says Danny.

"I think I did," I say.

"What are we going to do?"

"I don't know."

"Should we call the police?"

"I don't think that would be a good idea, Dan. They'll probably arrest *us* for pretending that we were going to be murdered in the first place."

"But we *are* going to be murdered!" says Danny.

"We weren't *then*," I say. "And if we shut up, then there is every chance that we won't be now."

"But how do we know for sure?" says Danny. "He's crazy. Did you see the look in his eyes?"

"He did seem a little high-strung," I say.

"High-strung!" says Danny. "That's putting it mildly. He was ready to flip out completely. I know. I've had a lot of experience with these guys."

"Oh, really?" I say. "When?"

"Just then!" says Danny.

"That's hardly a lot of experience."

"I watch TV. I can recognize a psycho when I see one. He's going to kill us . . . unless . . ."

"Unless what?" I say.

"Unless we strike first," says Danny.

"What are you suggesting?"

Danny just stares back at me. "Do I have to spell it out?"

SAY NO
TO LAND
MINES.

PAGE 106.

I cup my hands around each side of my mouth. "Earth to Danny! Do you read me — over?"

"You think I'm crazy?"

"I know it."

"Well, what do *you* suggest?" he says.

"I think if he's as stressed as he seems, then it would be a good idea to help him *de-stress*. Cut the problem off at the source."

"What have you got in mind?" says Danny. "Elephant tranquilizer darts?"

"I've got the next best thing," I say. "Meditation music."

"Meditation?" says Danny. "I've never heard of them."

"They're not a band, you idiot," I say. "It's just soft relaxing music. Jen's got tons."

I bound up the steps of the porch, go into the house, and head toward Jen's room.

Jen is going through this huge New Age thing at the moment. Ever since she went to the New Age & Psycho Expo, it's been meditation, chanting, incense, and soft music.

I'm sure she won't mind if I just borrow one of her tapes. And even if she does mind, she can just meditate and then she won't be angry anymore.

PAGE 117.

97

I open the door of her room.

I'm almost knocked backward by the stench.

There is a stick of incense burning in a holder on her dressing table. It smells like cat pee.

But it gives me an idea. I grab a handful of incense sticks from the bowl beside the holder. They might come in handy.

I pinch my nose and walk over to her tape collection.

WIN A FREE GARDEN GNOME (second-hand with paint peeling)

QUESTION continued...

on different continents one fueled by diesel, the other not. Which one will get to YEMEN first?

Write your answer on your bird and mail it to: GPO Box 1001100110011001100111

She has every type you can imagine: waterfall, birdcalls, rain forest, wind, breaking waves — you name it, she's got it. The only thing she hasn't got is breaking wind. I guess that's because breaking wind is not relaxing. It's too funny.

I choose a rain forest tape and head for the door before the smell of the incense makes me throw up all over her yin-and-yang rug.

On my way back outside, I go to my room and get my boom box. It's getting old, but it does the job. I just hope the batteries are up to it.

Danny is pacing up and down the backyard lawn.

"Where have you been?" he asks. "You've

Page 128.

98

been gone for ages! What if Mr. Broadbent had come back?"

"Relax, Danny. I've got a rain forest tape. By the time we're finished, the only thing Mr. Broadbent will be coming back to do is to hug us for making him feel so good."

"Yuck!" says Danny. "I don't think we should make him feel *that* good."

I set my tape player up on the porch. I insert Jen's tape and press play.

The music comes on. A long, low synthesizer note. It sounds like bird noises over the top, although it's hard to tell. It could be just the squeaking of the tape player's motor.

"Louder!" says Danny. "It's too soft."

"It's meant to be soft."

"Yeah, but Mr. Broadbent will never hear it. Turn it up."

Danny's right. I turn the volume up. It makes it louder, but kind of distorted as well.

"It doesn't sound very rain foresty," says Danny.

"I know, but it's better than nothing."

"Hey," says Danny, "what if we sprayed the hose onto Mr. Broadbent's roof? That might help."

But the story was dropped because it wasn't annoying enough.

BACKYARD OLYMPICS. EVENT 37

Fencing

(HOWL!)

Page 139. That's it book's over.

99

RAIN ON THE ROOF WHAT A BEAUTIFUL SOUND!

Why not? Rain on the roof is a very relaxing sound. How is Mr. Broadbent going to know it's not real?

I cross the yard to the faucet. The hose is not actually going to reach over to the fence because it's in a huge tangled knot from the last time I used it. And this is no ordinary knot. This is a knot that will take forever to untangle. And we haven't got forever. Mr. Broadbent could come storming up the driveway any second.

I turn the faucet on full blast and drag the hose as far as I can before the knot threatens to cut off the supply. The water makes it over the fence but not onto the roof.

"It's not going to work!" I yell.

"Tighten the nozzle!" calls Danny.

WOOF

A boxer.
(P.S. This
joke should
be on pg. 32.)

I screw the nozzle tighter. That's better. Especially if I point the hose up higher. It makes a perfect arc of water right onto the roof above Mr. Broadbent's office. A few minutes of rain on the roof combined with the rain forest tape will mellow Mr. Broadbent for sure.

It's risky, though. If the water pressure drops, the water will hit Mr. Broadbent's office window. He might think we're doing it to annoy him.

BOOM

Book's finished. You can all go home.

100

You've probably noticed my head is a finger.

Danny gives me the thumbs-up.

We're almost out of trouble.

But I don't want to take any chances.

Not when our lives are at stake.

I've still got the incense sticks.

I wave to Danny.

He comes over.

"Danny," I say. "I need you to light the bar-becue."

"You can eat?" he says. "At a time like this?"

"No," I say. "I'm not hungry. I want to use it to burn some incense. We can waft the smoke across to Mr. Broadbent's house. The smell will help to calm him even more."

"Anything is worth a try," says Danny. "What do I do?"

"Here," I say. I give him the incense. "Light the fire and then throw these on top. If we burn them all at once, it will be really intense."

"Where's the barbecue?"

"In the garage. But you'll need to wheel it closer to the fence."

Danny wheels the barbecue — half a fifty-five-gallon drum mounted on a frame with wheels — down to the other end of the drive-way, away from the hose spray. He grabs a

FAVORITE
INCENSE
FLAVORS

Pig's trotter.

Cow Manure.

Green Cheese.

Brussels Sprouts.

LIVE
GUM
LEAF

DEAD
GUM
LEAF

LIVE
MATCH

DEAD
MATCH

branch full of dead leaves from the garden and puts it in the top of the drum.

"Got a match?" asks Danny.

"Your face and a monkey's butt."

"Don't joke! This is serious."

"I'm not joking," I say.

Danny shakes his head. He falls for it every time.

"Just tell me where the matches are."

"They're under the barbecue."

He pulls the box out and lights a match. He drops it into the middle of the dead leaves. A thin white strand of smoke rises almost immediately.

"Quick!" I say. "Put the incense on top!"

Danny throws the incense on.

The leaves burst into flame, but the blaze is too strong. The smoke is going straight up into the air.

"It's not working, Danny. You need to fan the smoke across the fence."

"How?" he says.

"I dunno — use your shirt or something."

Danny pulls his T-shirt over his head. He starts flapping it wildly. The smoke billows around him. He coughs.

"Is it working?" he asks. "I can't see a thing."

TICK

We've all got homes to go to. Go on. Clear off.

Just call me the FINGER PRINCE.

"Not exactly," I say. "You'll have to fan harder."

Danny goes into fanning overdrive.

The smoke starts heading toward Mr. Broadbent's office.

"That's it, Danny! Keep going!"

I can just imagine Mr. Broadbent. He's probably sitting back with his feet on the desk. Arms behind his head. Eyes closed as he listens to the calming music and the relaxing rain. Taking deep breaths of soothing incense. Forgetting all about his work, his problems, and, most important, his threat to murder us.

Danny is piling more leaves onto the barbecue.

"Hang on, Danny, I think that's enough," I say.

But Danny doesn't hear me above the crackling of the fire. He keeps piling on more leaves. Showers of sparks fly into the air. The ends of half-burnt branches are falling to the ground. Danny keeps fanning.

"Danny! Stop it!"

His fanning is sending a torrent of sparks toward the fence. There's smoke everywhere.

Uh-oh. Just as I feared.

These are just the credits.

103

Not all of the smoke is coming from the barbecue.

Dad is always saying how he's going to pull the old dead passion-fruit vine off the back fence. Well, he won't have to bother now.

JUST ANNOYING ↓

"Danny! No more fanning! The vine is on fire."

Danny comes to his senses.

"Huh? What? Help!" he yells. "FIRE!"

I remember I'm holding the hose.

I point it toward the fire but it's too short to reach. I try to pull it closer but the water almost cuts off completely because of the tangle.

The flames are leaping high into the air. The whole fence will go up unless we do something fast.

"What do I do?" yells Danny.

There is a pile of fresh grass clippings on the other side of the driveway. They're only a couple of days old. They might help to damp the blaze.

"The grass clippings, Danny! Behind you! Throw them on the fire!"

Danny throws great armfuls of grass all over the fence and onto the barbecue.

It puts the fire out alright.

But now we have a new problem.

Trust me. 104

TICK TICK

Smoke.

Thick, white, eye-watering smoke.

My eyes are streaming.

A loud thrumming noise breaks the silence.

I look up and realize that I'm blasting the hose directly against Mr. Broadbent's office window.

Big mistake.

And the rain forest tape is starting to sound really weird. It's not only distorted, it's speeding up and slowing down as well.

Sooty is standing at the door of his kennel, barking.

Danny's still yelling. I can't make out what he's saying.

There's smoke and distorted music and yelling and barking, and the next thing I see is Mr. Broadbent's head — his eyes wide and bloodshot, his teeth bared — and his enormous hands reaching for me through the smoke.

ANGER!! How To IDENTIFY IT.

GLOWING CRANIUM

ROTATING EYEBALLS

NORMALLY BLUNT TEETH BECOME HARD, LONG & POINTY

STEAM FROM NOSTRILS

I don't think he wants to hug me, either.

"Do you want to talk?" I offer. "Talking through your problems can really help. . . ."

He doesn't respond.

I point the hose at him and let him have it. No use. It's like firing a water pistol at

I'm a PAGE NUMBER FLY.

SINGLE HANDED

DOUBLE HANDED

DOUBLE HANDED WITH DOG.

Godzilla. Mr. Broadbent just keeps coming — arms outstretched.

I want to run but I can't move. I'm too scared.

Just as Mr. Broadbent's hands are about to close around my neck, I see Danny charging up behind him.

He lets out a bloodcurdling yell and leaps onto Mr. Broadbent's back.

Mr. Broadbent roars. He knocks Danny off with one swipe and turns his attention back to me. Danny falls to the ground. He gets right back up and runs at Mr. Broadbent. Mr. Broadbent is unfazed. He simultaneously grabs Danny by the throat with his right hand and me by the throat with his left.

I look at Danny. Danny looks at me.

We nod.

We know exactly what to do.

We've practiced it many times.

We each take a deep breath and give it everything we've got.

"MURDER!" we yell. "MURDER, BLOODY MURDER!"

LANGUAGE, BLOODY LANGUAGE!

That's it... I'm out of here.

THE LAST JAFFA

I'm stewing.

James Bond is just about to be eaten by a shark and I'm going to miss it because I can't see past the hair of the woman in front of me.

BIG HAIR PERSON.

It doesn't matter where I sit in a movie theater, a person with a really big pile of hair on their head will always sit right in front of me. And if they don't, then the tallest person in the world will.

It's not fair. Nobody else has got a big-hair person in front of them. Why me?

DON'T BE FOOLED

"Hey, Danny," I say, "wanna swap seats?"

Danny is stuffing his mouth full of popcorn.

"Are you kidding?" he says, spitting little bits of popcorn all over me.

I'm glad I don't have popcorn. Popcorn is for kids. I've got a box of Jaffas. Well, to be more accurate, a box of *Jaffa* because there's only one left. One delicious chocolate candy with a tasty orange center.

"Forget it," I say. "Dad? Want to change seats?"

"Shush," he says. "James Bond is about to be eaten by a shark."

"I know," I say. "I'd really like to see it."

I know he's not really going to be eaten because he's James Bond and James Bond always escapes, but it's fun to watch how he does it. Well, it would be fun if I could see the screen.

I'd go and sit somewhere else, but the theater is packed.

"Who's that, Mommy?" says a little boy with a loud voice a couple of rows in front of us.

"A bad man."

"What's he doing, Mommy?"

"He's going to feed James Bond to the sharks."

"Why?"

"Because he's a bad man."

"Why?"

"Shh," she says, "Just watch."

BEWARE of
THE MANIAC
USHER

What kind of person would bring a little kid to a James Bond movie? I have enough trouble understanding all the double-crossings and plot twists myself, and I'm quite intelligent. Well, compared to Danny that is.

I can hardly see anything through all the hair. I lean over toward Danny.

This is one nasty bad man. He's got this trapdoor that falls open into a pool with a shark in it. If there's somebody he doesn't like, he just chains them up, hoists them above the pool, and dunks them in. James Bond's toes are only centimeters from the water.

The lady with the big hair tilts her head to the side.

I lean a little farther over toward Danny.
She tilts again.
I lean farther.
Danny elbows me in the ribs. He does it so hard that my Jaffa is knocked out of my fingers and falls to the floor.

"Keep on your side of the seat," he says.
"You idiot!" I hiss. "You made me drop my Jaffa."

"Have some popcorn," says Danny.
He shoves the box under my nose. I brush it away.

The Adventures of Jenni Jaffa

THE END.

You shouldn't be here. The book's finished.

IDENTIFYING
YOUR LOST
JAFFA

①

GRASP IT
FIRMLY
BETWEEN
THUMB AND
FOREFINGER.

②

Turn the
handle
marked
"HOT".

③

Engage the
4WD LEVER
and separate
the two
layers.

④

Kiss the
dog firmly
on the lips

⑤

PUT ON YOUR
HAT + COAT
AND LEAVE
THE SCENE
of the crime!
AS INNOCENTLY
AS POSSIBLE
... NOW!!

"No, you don't understand," I say. "That was my *last* Jaffa."

The lady with the big hair turns around.

"Shhh!" she says. "I'm trying to watch the movie."

"Tell me about it," I say under my breath.

"I beg your pardon?" she says.

"Nothing," I mumble.

I bend over and pat the floor all around me. No luck. It must have rolled into one of the rows in front.

This is terrible. Trapped behind a woman with big hair *and* I've lost my last Jaffa. And, to make things even worse, I missed seeing how James Bond got out of having his toes chomped by the sharks.

I slump down in my seat.

Life can be very cruel.

It's not like I can just go looking for the Jaffa.

The movie theater is packed. I'm in the middle of the center row. I would have to disturb nine people to get to the aisle. Besides, I can't just crawl down the center. It would attract too much attention. People might guess what I'm looking for. It might start a Jaffa-rush.

Can you please leave the book.

Safer just to sit here and sulk.

But then I think of how James Bond would react in this situation. He wouldn't just sit here. How did he put it? *A field operative must use every means at his disposal to achieve his objective.* He would go after the Jaffa and do whatever necessary to retrieve it — no matter how great the odds against him — no matter how dangerous.

EVERY MEANS AT HIS DISPOSAL.

I'm going to find that Jaffa.

Before I know it, I'm on my belly crawling commando-style underneath a row of movie-theater seats. The darkness makes it hard to see and the danger of accidentally touching somebody's leg is high. But I have to do it.

Go get 'em spotty.

I have a mission.

It's slow going. My body keeps sticking to the floor. There must be millions of cups of spilled Coke and 7-Up down here. Not to mention all the other stuff. Old popcorn buckets, ice-cream wrappers, drink cups, candy boxes, ripped-up movie tickets, used tissues . . . everything except my Jaffa.

Love is... sharing.

At the end of the aisle, I do a sort of somersault and slip into the next row. There is a forest of legs and shoes for as far as I can see.

Hang on.

I've got a job to do.

111

I can smell Jaffa.

I wriggle my way toward the smell and stop. It's directly above me.

I can see two small legs dangling over the edge of the seat.

It's the little kid with the big mouth. If anybody knows anything about my Jaffa, then he will. Kids and Jaffas go together like . . . well . . . kids and Jaffas.

I can hear cellophane crackling.

The sound of an engine fills the theater.

"Why is that man hanging from the air-plane?" says the boy.

"He's trying to catch the bad man," says his mother in a low voice.

"Why don't they stop and let him in?"

"Shhh!" says his mother. "Just watch."

"That's very dangerous, isn't it, Mommy?" says the boy.

"Shush!"

I roll onto my back. I push myself slowly into a position where I can see the boy. Just as I suspected. He's got Jaffas. I have an ex-cellent sense of smell.

He's holding them in his left hand. They are resting on the seat beside his knee. The box is almost full. I can see a Jaffa poking out of the top.

I could just reach up and take it. Just one. It's not my lost one, but it would do. The kid won't mind. He won't even know. He's staring at the screen. It's a low thing to steal candy from children. Very low. James Bond would never do that. I would never do that.

I'm just going to borrow it.

I raise my hand toward the Jaffa. My thumb and forefinger are poised, like a cobra about to strike. The Jaffa is almost mine.

"Mommy," says the kid in a loud voice, "why is there a boy under my seat?"

I pull my hand back and wriggle back undercover. Bigmouth strikes again!

"Shhh!" says his mother. "Don't be so silly."

"But, Mom," he says, "there's a boy under my seat."

"I've told you before," she says, "stop telling stories."

My cover's been blown! I have to get out of the danger zone. Fast.

I take off down the aisle, elbows pumping. I bump my head. I burn my knees. I knock my shoulders. But I keep going until I can't go any farther. I'm caught on a strap. It's pulled tight under my arm. At the end of the strap, I can see a purse. And that's not all. The strap is looped around a woman's ankle.

"Hey!" says a voice. A hand with long fingernails reaches down and starts tugging on the strap. "Help! Someone's trying to steal my purse. Help!"

But the harder she pulls the strap, the harder it is to unhook it from my shoulder.

I flop onto my back and push myself out from under the seat to help slip the strap off my arm.

It works. My arm is free.

But now I have an even bigger problem. Someone is shrieking.

"Eeek! What are you doing?!!"

It takes me a moment to realize that I'm looking up the dress of the woman in the next seat.

Not that I am looking. I'm not. I'm just trying to get rid of the purse strap. But it's going to be hard to explain the difference. James Bond would know how to do it, but when it comes to the crunch, I'm no James Bond. It's safer and easier just to scram.

on Pg 114 You idiot!

114

I pull my head back under the seat and start the long journey back to where I started. Operation Find-the-Lost-Jaffa has been aborted. I'll be happy just to find my seat.

Too late.

I can see a white flashlight beam sweeping across the carpet.

A security guard!

I can't go forward and I can't go back.

He stops at the end of my aisle.

He is wearing black leather shoes. The shoelaces are tied in big floppy bows. The toes are scuffed. Probably from kicking trouble-makers like me out of the movie theater.

"What's the problem?" calls the guard.

"Thief!" gasps the purse woman.

"Sicko!" says the woman sitting next to her.

"Who me?" says the guard.

"No, under the seat!" says the purse woman.

"Which one?" says the guard.

I'm breathing hard. Heart thudding.

Any minute now, he's going to shine the flashlight under the seat.

Unless . . .

Brainstorm!

WIN FABULOUS PRIZES!! (continued from Pg 73)

...A FROZEN CHICKEN SKATE BOARD.

How lucky can you be?

FOOL PROOF
KNOT FOR
TYING AN
ENEMY'S
SHOELACES
TOGETHER.
① Take your
partner

by the hand
② Be firm

but gentle

③

④ Relax
and reload.

Now don't get me wrong. Tying some-body's shoelaces together is on par with steal-ing candy from children. It's not an activity that I would normally have any part of or rec-ommend to others. But this is an emergency. After all, a field operative must use every means at his disposal to achieve his objective.

I reach out and pluck the end of the guard's shoelace from its loose knot. It unties easily. The lace of his other shoe comes undone just as easily. I tie the two laces together in a sim-ple slip knot. I brace myself. This is it. I spread my fingers apart like I'm steadying myself for the start of a hundred-yard sprint.

That's weird.

I can feel something underneath my right hand.

It's small and hard. And round.

Hang on!

I don't believe it.

My Jaffa! I've found it.

Against incredible odds.

I put it in my pocket.

James Bond would be proud of me. I steady myself and prepare to bolt.

"Which row?" asks the guard.

"This row!" scream the women in unison.

11.

The guard bends down and shines his flashlight right in my face.

"Good evening!" I say in my suavest James Bond voice and then launch myself right at him and into the aisle.

In his surprise, the guard steps backward. And falls. Ouch!

The flashlight goes flying.

I'm out in the center aisle. But in all the excitement, I can't remember where I was sitting.

I could yell "hellooo!" and hope that Danny replies, but that wouldn't be too smart. Everyone would know where I am.

There is one way, though.

It's not going to be pleasant but I have to do it. Only my uncanny sense of smell can help me now.

I empty my lungs. I close my eyes. I breathe in through my nose, searching for a particular smell. A particularly bad smell. The worst smell in the whole world. A smell that's kind of a cross between bad breath, dog pooh, and garlic.

Danny's foot odor.

Lucky for me, Danny has a habit of taking his shoes off in the movie theater. Judging by

11

the smell, it must be about the only time he ever does take them off.

Got it! Two rows back to the middle and nine seats across.

Just in time. At least a half dozen flashlight beams start streaming down the aisles.

Backup security!

I throw myself toward the aisle where the stench is the strongest and dive under the seats before the flashlight beams hit.

JUST ANNOYING? I don't think so.

I move smoothly until I get to a seat without any legs in front of it. That must be mine. I emerge and slip back into my place as if nothing has happened.

"Right on!" says Danny.

"Shut up!" I say. "Just act normal."

The guards are patrolling the theater like it's a prison.

I pretend to be absorbed by the movie.

It's not easy. I've completely lost track of what's going on. And I still can't see the screen properly.

All I can make out is that James Bond and his girlfriend are trapped in this enormous factory. It's filled with smoke and fire. Explosions left, right, and center. They are desperately pressing buttons to get the doors open.

My Jaffa!

I have to eat the Jaffa before I lose it again.

I put the Jaffa in my mouth. This is going to be good. I worked for this. I deserve it.

That's funny. I didn't know they made Jaffas with a mint center. And so chewy.

That's not right. It's not a Jaffa. It's somebody's old chewing gum.

I clutch at my throat. What if the person who last chewed that gum was really sick and now I've got some horrible disease?

I spit the gum out.

It flies through the air, straight into the hair of the woman in front of me.

She jumps up.

"There's something in my hair!" she screams. "Urgh! Chewing gum."

She turns to me and points.

"You did this, you nasty little boy!"

I slump down in my seat.

The purse woman stands up. "That's the boy who tried to steal my purse!"

The other woman is beside her.

"He tried to look up my dress!"

"No!" I say to them. "You're making a terrible mistake. That was just somebody who *looks* like me!"

BEWARE of
ANCIENT
BITS OF
GUM.
favorite
disguises:

1.

As
old JAFFA.

2.

As
innocent
baby's
pacifier.

3.

As
CASHEW
NUT

4.

As pills.

5

As usher's
right
eyebrow.

There's
a lot of
Page 11's
in this
book.

11

Guards everywhere. More and more people are crowding around my seat. Nobody seems to be interested in the movie anymore.

Even the little kid is standing on his seat and pointing.

"That's him," he says, "See, Mommy! That's the boy who was under my seat."

His mother stands up.

"Is this true?" she says.

Before I can answer, the first guard is shining his flashlight in my face.

"It's you!" he says. "The one who tied my shoelaces together!"

The faces of these people appear twisted and evil in the half-light of the movie theater. The guard is a dead ringer for the villain in the film.

I turn to Danny for support.

"Tell them I'm innocent, Danny! Tell them!" I plead.

But Danny's seat is empty. So is Dad's.

They've abandoned me. I can't say I blame them. This is one ugly mob.

"Hey, look, I'm sorry," I say. "I'd love to stay and chat but I have to be going. . . ."

"Stay right there," says the guard. "You're in big trouble!"

BEWARE OF
ANCIENT
BITS OF
GUM.

- They will attach themselves to unsuspecting persons.

- They will seek out the moist passages in the body.

- Slowly but surely they will make their way to the brain.

- Gradually they will take over the host's personality and appearance

Pg 12. That's more like it.

12

He pushes me back down into my seat.

"Let's harpoon him!" says the purse lady. People cheer.

"Feed him to the sharks!" cries the dress lady.

Even more cheering.

"Wait a minute," says a voice. "Does anybody have a harpoon or a shark?"

People go quiet. They shake their heads.

On the screen, James Bond has just set a man on fire with a cigarette lighter.

"Let's set him on fire!" cries someone else. "I've got a lighter."

"Not in my theater you don't," says an usher. "I'm the one who has to clean up after this."

These people are obviously crazy. Too much James Bond. I have to get out of here.

"Look up there!" I yell, pointing at the roof. "Ninjas!"

Everybody looks. They're so James Bonded–out that they'll believe anything.

It's the chance I need to heave myself out of my seat. But this time, I'm not going un- der — I'm going over. Over the head of the big-hair woman. I use her shoulders as a springboard to leap across two rows into an

ANCIENT PIECE of GUM lies in wait for an unsuspecting shoe to attach itself to.

BEWARE.

Belt of
M+M's
↓

CHUPA CHOP

TWISTIE

JAFFA

FANTAILS

Aniseed
balls
THE CANDY
UNIVERSE

empty seat. I use the seat as a trampoline to propel me across another three rows.

An old man tries to hook me around the ankle with the handle of his cane. But I grab the cane and use it to polevault across the last two rows of seats and up onto the narrow platform in front of the screen.

I look around. Nowhere to go. Both of the front exits are blocked by guards. And the mob is closing in.

What now? What would James Bond do? He would use every means at his disposal to achieve his objective, of course. If I can't go forward and I can't go sideways, that only leaves one direction. Backward. Into the screen!

The hands of the mob are clutching at my feet.

No time to lose.

I jump backward.

There is an incredible ripping and tearing noise and then everything goes quiet.

It's time
you were
in bed.

Next thing I know I'm lying on a wooden floor.

Someone's
tampering
with my
numbers

12

I can hear cheering and whistling. It's coming from the other side of the screen.

And then I see it. My Jaffa.

And not just my Jaffa. There's hundreds and thousands of Jaffas and old candy! All the candy that has ever been hurled at the screen or lost in the history of this movie theater has ended up here.

THE
RETURN
OF
THE LAST
JAFFA.

And they're mine.

All mine.

I pick my Jaffa up off the floor. I wipe the dust off it and put it into my mouth. No minty taste this time. Just pure Jaffa.

I reach for another. And another. And another.

My only problem now is how I'm going to eat all this candy without being sick.

It's going to be tough.

But I can handle it.

A field operative must use every means at his disposal to achieve his objective.

I'll think of something.

STOP
DOING
THAT!

SWINGING ON THE CLOTHESLINE

f you've never tried swinging on the clothesline at night, then you should. I recommend it.

I've been out here every night for the past three weeks. From midnight to 4:00 A.M.

But not for fun. I'm in training. I'm going to set a new world record for the fastest-ever clothesline swinging. It's my dream.

Unfortunately, my parents don't share my dream. That's why I have to do my training at night while they're asleep. Whenever they catch me swinging on the clothesline, they go berserk. I've tried to explain to them that I'm not just fooling around, that I'm trying to achieve something special, but it's no use.

"Why can't you play a normal sport like

9 out of 10 school principals confess:
At the end of another stressful school day, we take a bit of relief on the school clothesline.

soccer?" says Dad. "Something that takes real skill."

Real skill?

Now don't get me wrong. I've got nothing against soccer, but anyone can play it. All you need to know is how to run and kick at the same time.

But breaking the world speed-swinging record — now that takes real skill, real dedication, and real guts. You need to combine an exhaustive knowledge of aerodynamics with a thorough understanding of the mechanics of spinning clotheslines. You also need to be fit enough to withstand G-forces stronger than most NASA astronauts will ever have to endure. Not to mention being able to run fast when your parents see you. That's what I call *real* skill.

The bar is cold under my fingers. The wind is cool. There is a slight frost in the air. If I tilt my head back, I can see the stars circling above me.

I'm swinging faster and faster. I feel good. I can hear the *squeak-squeak-squeak* of the clothesline as I spin. I take one hand off the bar and readjust my goggles. Yes, I know that swimming goggles are not the coolest look in

COPHIN
BROTHERS,
FUNERAL
DIRECTORS,
ADMIT:

We do
it, too

After a
busy day
funeral
directing,
we go home,
into the back-
yard and
fly on the
clothesline.

weeee

the world, but it gets pretty hard to see at the speeds I get up to.

I hear the back door slam.

Uh-oh.

The floodlight comes on and the yard is bathed in bright white light.

Dad is standing there in his bath robe.

"What do you think you're doing?" he yells.

I thought it was fairly obvious, but with parents you can never quite tell. Sometimes they see things very differently than normal people. Best to keep it simple.

"Swinging on the clothesline, Dad. I'm training."

"Training? I'll give you training!"

Dad grabs hold of the straw broom leaning next to the steps and comes rushing at me with it raised above his head.

I don't think "training" is exactly what he has in mind. I think "thrashing" would be closer to the mark.

I haven't got time to get away. This is going to take a bit of fancy footwork. I rock myself back and forth to work up as much extra speed as I can. I wait until Dad is right beside the line. Just as he is about to swing

126
3276.
WHAT!

126 3276

the broom at me, I assume my best Bruce Lee pose and kick the broom out of his hand.

The broom goes flying.

I release my grip on the line, do a spectacular double somersault dismount, and hit the ground running.

I sprint up the steps into the house and into the safety of my bedroom.

I push my dressing table in front of the door.

"Open up, Andy!" says Dad. "I want to talk to you."

He's rattling the door handle.

"Can't it wait until the morning?" I say. "I'm trying to sleep."

"No, it can't," says Dad. He throws himself against the door like some TV cop trying to break down the door of a TV criminal.

After ten minutes, he gives up.

"I'll see you in the morning," he says, making it sound like the biggest threat in the world. But that suits me fine. By then he'll have cooled down. He might even have come to realize just how serious I am.

I put my head on the pillow and dream of how proud Mom and Dad will be when I set the new world record. They'll come into the

BACKYARD OLYMPICS EVENT 46:

The REVERSE UPSIDE DOWN TOE HANG.

Competitor pegs big toe to clothesline.

Competitor must hang upside down face out and spin. Last to fall...wins.

NOTE: To save embarrassment you should glue your shirt to your skin.

I'll HOLD MY BREATH.

127 AEC

kitchen and the newspaper will be on the table with the headline: "BOY BREAKS WORLD CLOTHESLINE SPEED RECORD!" There'll be a big picture of me swinging on a clothesline in the middle of a huge stadium packed with cheering fans. And I'll just be sitting there eating my breakfast, real cool, and Mom and Dad will be overwhelmed and they'll get down on their knees and beg my forgiveness for not taking my ambition seriously and for placing so many obstacles in my way. . . . But I won't hold a grudge. I'll just wave my hand, dab at my mouth with a napkin, stand up, and say, "Hey — no hard feelings. . . . we all make mistakes. Now if you'll excuse me, I have to go and get ready for the street parade that the prime minister is putting on in my honor . . ."

WORLD RECORD NUMBER OF PEOPLE ON A CLOTHES-LINE

27 + 1 dog.

The scene that greets me at the breakfast table the next morning is a little different.

Dad is sitting there with an expression on his face like one of those Easter island statues.

The radio, which is usually burbling away, is not turned on.

KNOCK KNOCK

The sound of my cornflakes clattering into

I'm holding my breath

128.7 FM

my bowl sounds like a hundred tons of boulders falling on top of the kitchen.

"We're very disappointed in you, Andy," says Dad.

"Yes, Dad."

"You've let us down."

"Yes, Dad."

"I've had to buy three new clotheslines this year, and do you know why?"

"Because they're really bad quality?" I suggest.

Dad's ears start wiggling. Wrong answer.

"No!" he yells. "Because the others were so mangled and broken from your infernal swinging."

I still think it's a quality issue. If he would buy top-of-the-line, superstrength clotheslines, instead of these ones made out of nothing stronger than coat hanger wire, then we wouldn't have a problem. But I don't say this. Dad is in no mood to see reason. Besides, he's not finished yet.

"Your mother and I have begged you, have pleaded with you, have extracted promises from you — have even bribed you — to stop swinging on the clothesline, but to no avail. I thought we got things straight the last time

CSA
Clothesline
Swingers
Anonymous

Hello, my
name is
Zelda
Sparrow,
I'm 63 year
old and I
am a
Clothesline
Swinger.

Average
Lifespan
of Andy's
Promises?
A ... 15min
B ... 1 day
C ... 4000yrs
Answer below

If you
answered ©
you are correct.
Andy is VERY
trustworthy.
If you picked ⒶⒷⒸ
you are obviously
a parent.

GASP! 129 x 7 =

$$\begin{array}{r} 129 \\ \times\ 7 \\ \hline 903 \end{array} \checkmark$$

we talked, but now we discover that you are sneaking out there in the middle of the night. What have you got to say for yourself?"

"I have a dream . . ." I say.

"You have a what?" interrupts Dad.

"Nothing," I say. What's the point of even talking about it? I've explained it a hundred times and they still don't get it.

I push my cornflakes toward the center of the table and stand up.

"I'm not really hungry," I say. "I've got to get to school."

"Not so fast," says Dad. "This is the last time I intend to have this conversation. Swinging on the clothesline must stop, and if you think you're going to find that too difficult, then don't worry. I will make it very easy for you."

"What do you mean?" I say.

"You'll see," he says with a smile. "You'll see."

That's what he thinks.

Nothing is going to stop my training. I'm just hitting my peak. What's the worst he can do?

Sit out there all night on guard with a

130

broom across his legs? He'll need to sleep sometime.

Electrify the line? I'll wear a rubber suit.

Set up a Super Soaker to spray the line with water when it's triggered by a motion sensor? I'll wear raingear.

Nothing will stop me.

I'll see? I don't think so. We'll see who'll see.

That afternoon, when I get home from school, I walk up the driveway and into the backyard.

Suddenly a huge black dog comes bar-relling toward me.

It's massive. Snarling. Long white strings of foam trailing from its bared teeth. And it's heading straight for me.

I clutch the straps of my bag and get ready to bop it on the head. It's not much — like trying to scare off a charging bull with a rolled-up towel — but it's all I've got.

The dog lunges for me, but just as it's about to sink its fangs into my neck it is tugged violently backward. It rears up on its hind legs and flips over onto its back. It has reached the end of its chain, which — as I collect myself — I notice is attached to the clothesline.

QUEEN COMES CLEAN!

I got up to MACH 5 on our HILLS Hoist last week.

I hear laughter from the porch.

"Andy," says Dad, "I'd like you to meet Spot. Spot, this is Andy."

Spot picks himself up from the ground. He lunges at me again.

I jump backward.

"Are you crazy?" I ask Dad. "That dog's a killer!"

GRRRR

"Spot? A killer?" says Dad. "Nah. He's harmless. He just gets a bit touchy when people go too close to the clothesline."

"You've bought this dog just to stop me from swinging on the clothesline?" I say.

"I haven't bought him," says Dad. "I just arranged a little swap."

Make my day, kid.

"You swapped him for Sooty?"

"Not permanently."

"For how long?"

"For as long as it takes you to break your clothesline habit and develop some new, more healthy interests," says Dad.

"Like soccer you mean?"

KNOCK

132

"Yes, like soccer — like other boys."

"I'm not like other boys!" I yell. "I need something more challenging."

"Well," says Dad, "I think you'll find Spot challenging enough."

I look at Spot.

He's straining on his leash. Staring at me. Just daring me to take one step toward his clothesline.

I've got to admit that at this moment, soccer is starting to look pretty attractive. I'd even consider taking up golf.

I turn around and go back down the driveway to enter the house by the front door.

I throw my bag hard against my bedroom wall. My pencil case falls out, and pencils go flying all over the floor. I pick up a handful and throw them against the window.

Just when the speed record was within my grasp!

From my bedroom window I can see Spot. He is sitting straight-backed, ears twitching, ready to tear apart anyone who is even thinking about going near the clothesline.

Fifty pounds of prime slobbering dog power.

BACKYARD OLYMPICS EVENT 8:

CHICKEN CHASE.

1. Let out all of your next door neighbor's chickens.

2. Allow them 5 mins to settle

3. Now try to get them into his back door. (This is best done while he is out) (The key is under the plaster frog)

The world record for getting 12 chickens into the kitchen of a next door neighbor is 22 mins.

Good Luck.

If only his power could be harnessed for good instead of evil.

Hang on — that's it!

In the early days of my training, I used to get Danny to tie a rope to one corner of the clothesline and tow me around at super-speeds. That was before I was able to generate them for myself and go faster than even Danny could run. But I'm looking at a dog with energy to burn.

If I could slip a harness around Spot and get him to pull me around, I could set a new world record yet. I'll show them!

It's 10:00 P.M.

Dad is in the kitchen.

"I think I'll go to bed early," he calls loud enough for me to hear. "I expect I'll sleep well without the creaking of the clothesline to wake me up — heh-heh-heh! Anyone for a cup of cocoa before bed?"

"Yes, please," says Mom.

It's the cue I've been waiting for. The noise of the kettle will block out any noise I make while I'm setting up.

3 STEP DOG HYPNOSIS:
1. Make the dog comfy.
2. Feed him a bowl of warm custard. (Do not put sleeping pills in the custard) (which you can get from the chemist.)
3. Read him your principal's address from the last school assembly. (if this doesn't work, tell him your life story).

It's a PAGE NUMBER FLY!

Are they rare?

I grab my equipment. Swimming goggles, Sooty's leash and a stuffed toy cat that I borrowed from Jen's room.

I tiptoe down the steps.

Spot is lying with his head on his forelegs.

He might be asleep. It's hard to tell. Are guard dogs allowed to sleep?

I take a step toward him.

He doesn't move.

I take another step.

He remains asleep.

Too easy!

I take another step. I'm now within his range.

He could wake up and chomp me in half, but am I scared?

You bet.

I place my foot down on the ground as carefully as if I was walking on a one-millimeter-thin piece of glass.

My right knee is shaking out of control.

I stoop down to steady it with my hand.

But my hand is shaking as well.

I try to steady my hand with my other hand. But that's shaking even worse. All the stuff drops onto the ground.

HOW A KNEE SHAKES

he he

KNEES SHAKE WHEN THEY HAVE BEEN INFILTRATED BY KNEEMATODES. A KNEEMATODE IS A TINY INSECT THAT HIDES BEHIND THE KNEECAP AND WOBBLES YOUR BONES JUST TO ANNOY YOU.

CATAPULT.

As hens' teeth.

Spot opens his eyes.

I can tell by his growl that he is not pleased to see me.

My whole body is shaking.

I pick up the fluffy cat and wave it in front of Spot's face. He is mesmerized. I throw the cat to one corner of the clothesline.

Spot is torn.

One eye on the cat. One eye on me.

I'm at his mercy, but I'm counting on the fact that not even years of specialist guard-dog training can overcome a dog's natural urge to chase cats.

I'm right.

Spot lunges at the cat.

There is an explosion of white fluff.

Better that than an explosion of me.

I loop the end of Sooty's leash over the corner of the clothesline above Spot. He's in a frenzy, tearing the remains of the cat apart.

This is my chance.

I sneak up behind him. I grab his neck chain and clip Sooty's leash on to it.

I run to the opposite corner of the line, jump up, and hold on.

Spot is still more interested in mangling the cat than in me.

"Hey, Spot," I call. "Your father was a sewer rat and your mother was a chihuahua!"

That gets his attention.

He looks up, rears up on his hind legs, and starts chasing me.

The line takes off with a *whoosh*!

Spot is going crazy. They must have starved him for weeks. Either that or he has taken an even greater offense at my insult than I could have predicted.

Whatever the reason, I am swinging faster than I have ever swung in my life.

I'm gripping the bar as tightly as I can. I feel like Superman — arms straight out, head down. I'm going so fast that I'm practically horizontal. The wind is roaring in my ears. I wish I'd thought to put more clothes on. I'm freezing.

The familiar landmarks of the backyard are gone — the shed, the old tree stump, the window of the kitchen where Mom and Dad are probably sipping their cocoa right at this moment. It's all just a blur of spinning color.

Spot is huffing and barking as he chases me around.

Any moment now, Mom and Dad are going to hear the racket. They are going to look

BACKYARD OLYMPICS EVENT 15

HOSE CHOPPING (mechanical)

1. Start up mower.

2. Lay hose on lawn in Pattern A. (see BACKYARD OLYMPIC MANUAL)

3. Pick one path and mow through hose.

4. Count how many pieces the hose is in now.

WORLD RECORD: 342. Mrs Valda Jones, Rockbank, Vic, Aust. (accidental)

HI MUM.

out of the kitchen window and see me spinning faster than any human being has spun before.

They'll see.

They'll see that I'm serious and that nothing will stop me.

But they're going to have to look soon, because the faster I go, the harder it is to hold on. It's like being caught in a tornado.

I can't keep this up much longer.

I'm not used to this sort of pressure.

My fingers give out.

I'm flying through the air.

Straight toward the kitchen window.

I'm wondering whether it's safer to crash through a window headfirst or break it with a fist, Superman-style.

It doesn't really matter, I guess.

If the window doesn't kill me, my parents will.